The Five Friends
Battle Against Aliens

The Five Friends
Battle Against Aliens
A Novel

Kiran Kumar Singh

AUTHORSPRESS

Worldwide Circulation through Authorspress Global Network
First Published in 2021
by
Authorspress
Q-2A Hauz Khas Enclave, New Delhi-110 016 (India)
Phone: (0) 9818049852
E-mail: authorspressgroup@gmail.com
Website: www.authorspressbooks.com

The Five Friends Battle Against Aliens
(A Novel)

ISBN 978-93-90588-02-2

Printed in India at Thomson Press (India) Limited

DEDICATION

In memory of my mother Mrs. Suraj Kumari and my wife Mrs. Reba Singh. The former retired as Professor and head of the Education Department of a reputed college and the latter was a qualified and talented artist. May their souls rest in peace.

FOREWORD

This is a science fiction adventure story featuring five small children and how they struggle to save the world from the clutches of powerful alien beings. They are guided by a good alien being who gives them magical powers. It is meant primarily for children and young adults but is suitable for all age groups including the elderly who are young at heart.

ACKNOWLEDGEMENT

This is to thank my sister Ms. Preeti Singh, M.A., M.Ed., M. Phil., and an excellent teacher of English language and literature. She read the entire manuscript and made meticulous corrections and gave excellent suggestions. I also thank my son Siddhartha for editing the manuscript.

CONTENTS

PROLOGUE

It was a dark night when the greatest evil being of the universe landed on a remote mountain peak in Peru bringing his four assistants whom he addressed as Numero Uno, Dos, Tres and Cuatro. They in turn called him the Boss. On landing on terra firma they all took human shape. The Boss had considerable magical powers, could travel billions of light years in the blink of an eyelid, and all five of them were immortal.

They went about their task of enslaving the human race by using their magical powers to control the minds of many people from the surrounding area and arming them with magical guns. Soon South America was under their absolute control and they were preparing to conquer the whole world. This would have dire consequences for the human race. The Boss would gradually drain the mental energy of all human beings till they were reduced to the level of animals. Then he would travel with his assistants to some other planet harboring intelligent life and repeat the same process there.

Fortunately, the greatest good being of the universe arrived on the earth to thwart their evil intentions. He also acquired human shape and called himself the Chimp because of a slight resemblance to that creature. Since the laws of nature did not permit direct conflict between these two great beings, the Chimp searched to enlist suitable humans to battle against the evil invaders. After considerable effort, he decided that a group of five young American children from the small town of

Bentonville were best suited for this purpose. All of them were very brave and highly talented. One night the Chimp appeared mysteriously in bedroom of one of children to enlist him and his friends to fight against the evil invaders.

❖❖❖

Chapter 1

THE MYSTERIOUS VISITOR

A group of children were playing softball in a clearing, near a forest on the edge of Bentonville, a small town near Seattle. There were only five of them, so they played a modified version of the game. These were no ordinary children. In their school they were better than any of the other children in studies, games and sports. They were very good friends and had a tremendous team spirit. Once they decided on doing something, there was no letting up till they completed it.

Their leader was Henry James Taylor, a brown haired, hazel eyed, good natured boy of twelve. He was a computer wizard, and very good at most other things also. His friendly nature and willingness to take responsibility made him a born leader.

Then there was Marie Delphine Bisset also twelve, with light brown hair and eyes, and pretty little dimples on her cheeks, which became larger whenever she smiled, which she did quite a bit. She was as competitive as any of the other four at any game or sport, and considered herself to be braver than any of them. She could hold her own in any argument and always got the last word. Being of French descent, she could read and write the language well. When annoyed she spoke English sarcastically with a French accent.

The third was John Martin Carver, a well-built athletic, African American boy, with large dark eyes, and a friendly smile and a helpful attitude. Like Henry, he too was a good leader. He had a keen interest in detective work and considered himself to be cut out for this line.

The fourth was Robert Warren Bruce, a well-built boy, slightly on the plump side due to his strong liking for good food. That did not make him physically unfit. In fact, he could run almost as fast as the others and was quite agile, considering his bulk. Like Henry, he too had a keen interest in computers, and was good at most things.

Last, but not the least, was Diego Ramon Gonzalez, a stocky boy, with dark hair and piercing black eyes. His grandparents were Spanish speaking immigrants, and he knew the language quite well, and spoke English like any other American kid. Like Marie, he too spoke English with an accent when annoyed, but his was a Spanish accent, and like John, he dreamt of becoming a detective or spy. The children soon became bored of playing softball. Marie said, "Somehow it is not as much fun playing the game as it used to be earlier."

"You are right," said John. "Nothing seems to be as much fun anymore."

"I guess, we are all worried about what happened In South America," said Robert. "It makes me worried."

"It is not only South America. Some strange things are going on here," said Diego. "I can't pinpoint it, but something creepy is going on. The birds don't sing as they used to and the flowers don't smell as they should. I won't be surprised if what happened in South America happens here."

"Oh, come on now! That's your imagination working overtime," said Henry. "It's the effect of brooding too much over

South America. This is a different place altogether. I can't imagine guerrillas charging out of the mountains to capture the country. Let's call it a day. We all have to go home and work on our computer projects."

Although Henry had dismissed what Diego had said, he too was immensely worried. Later that night he sat in front of his computer trying to concentrate and type his project. He knew he had to start soon, otherwise there was no way he could meet the Friday dead line, and also hope to get an A grade. His fingers itched to start typing on the keyboard, but his mind was distracted by the troubling events that were happening in the world. "I must start typing the project report," he muttered to himself, but it was of no use. That very evening, he had heard his parents discussing the troubling world news. He might be a little boy, only 12 years old, but he was far wiser, and more sensible than any child of his age. He was keenly aware of world events, and his brain was weighed down with worry over what had been happening.

The world was passing through a phase of dramatic changes. Within a short period of time the whole of South America had been taken over by armed bands of guerrillas. Country after country had fallen to them like nine pins, with Peru being the first to fall, followed by Uruguay, Bolivia, Chile and all of the others with Brazil and Argentina being among the last to fall. The world had never before witnessed such a chain of events.

These countries were now ruled by dictators, who had taken glorified titles: one being known as Generalissimo, another went by the title of Field Marshal, and another was simply El Liberator. Earlier they had been senior army officers with little or no interest in politics. Now they had glorified lives, with a lot of pomp and show. Apparently they were authoritarian rulers, but were puppets in the hands of a very powerful and evil alien master, who had come from some other world.

The rest of the world had rather vague reports about how it all happened, and who were the new rulers. Some newspapers and TV news channels carried sensational reports about the guerrilla forces armed with very accurate, rapid firing, ray guns with which they overwhelmed the policemen and soldiers, who tried to oppose them. Some reported that these guns emitted some kind of invisible ray, which could penetrate even thick walls and metal without damaging them. Many soldiers sitting inside their tanks were knocked unconscious or even killed, while the same happened to men and women inside their homes. The rays emitted by the guns didn't even leave a scratch on walls or the skins of the people knocked out or killed.

South America had now declared itself as the Union of Liberated South American Republics (ULSAR). All diplomatic relations with countries outside ULSAR had been broken, even though war was not declared. All travel and trade and normal communications abroad were stopped by the new puppet leaders of ULSAR, which had become like an island cut off from the rest of the world. No ships were allowed to come to their ports, no airplanes were allowed to land, and none were allowed to even fly over their territory.

There was only one form of communication with the world outside, and that was propaganda through radio broadcasts and TV transmissions. These were soul stirring messages to the populations to liberate themselves by overthrowing their corrupt governments. The joys of life in the newly created ULSAR and their new religion were publicised. The various news channels excelled each other in singing the praises of their new leaders, and the new religion that the people had adopted. All other countries of the world couldn't come to grips with the situation, as everything had happened too fast, and the absence of reliable news added to the confusion and indecision.

Most of the ambassadors, diplomats and other foreigners had fled, when it was apparent that the guerillas were about to take over. Those who remained were forced out by the new governments. Now and then, small groups of refugees managed to escape by motor boats or yachts or row boats, and brought some news about what was happening in this great continent. Their accounts of what was happening, were contradictory and only served to create confusion, and it was suspected that many of these people might be enemy agents sent to mislead and create confusion. With so much to worry about, it was not surprising that Henry could make no progress with his report. Then his thought strayed to the happenings in Africa, Australia, Asia, Europe and North America.

Strange events were taking place even in USA, which was the most frustrating of all. A few members of the president's own party were siding with the opposition party to oppose him. This had a paralysing effect on the government. The same story was unfolding in the states, the cities, the towns and the villages as well the labor unions. The highways and roads were in a poor state of repair. Airlines and trains were not running on time. Even garbage collection was irregular.

What was worse, even his own little town of Bentonville was affected. The mayor's office and police department were not being run effectively. He felt that the town which used to be such a cheerful and neat place had become dull and untidy. The birds did not sing like earlier and the flowers had lost their fragrance. It was as if the whole town was covered by a pall of gloom. His friends Robert, Diego, Marie and John were also affected by these changes. They talked often about these matters, but there was nothing they could do except feel worried and frustrated.

Marie was so unhappy that the others felt she might get depressed, and tried their best to keep her in good spirits.

Again he tried to get back to his report, and turned towards the computer, but at that very instant a sheet of paper came out of the screen edgewise. Then it rotated slowly through ninety degrees and he could make out that it had an outline drawing of a chimpanzee like figure with a smiling face. It remained suspended in the air for a few second and gradually morphed into a 3D being which seemed to be a human with a chimpanzee like build and facial look. The whole process lasted less than a minute. Henry sat rooted in his chair out of sheer fright and bewilderment. He wasn't sure whether it was a hallucination or a nightmare, and was about to run away when the figure spoke in a soothing tone, "Henry, don't be frightened. I mean no harm to you. I have come as a friend to talk with you about these things you were thinking about."

"Who or what are you, and how did you come out of the computer screen on a piece of paper as a drawing, and how on earth did you change yourself into a living being? How do you know my name, and what I was thinking about?" Henry blurted out.

"Not so fast. That's a lot of questions you have asked. I am the Computer Imp, but you can call me Chimp since I have a slight resemblance to a chimpanzee. I know a lot about you. You are Henry James Taylor, twelve years old, studying in Bentonville middle school in the fifth grade. You got your first name from your grandfather and the middle name from your father. Your mother and sister are Marian and Joan. Now you sit down and relax, while I tell you a story that will more or less answer your questions."

❖❖❖

Chapter 2

A STRANGE TALE

The Chimp sat down on Henry's bed, while the latter swiveled his chair around to face him and said, "I am ready to hear your story."

"It is the story of good versus evil. Both have existed since the creation of the universe and have been in conflict ever since. There have been long periods when evil dominated and then periods when good prevailed. The leader of all evil forces is someone whom I have named Demon Jaguar. It is my responsibility to motivate people, so that they can fight against Demon Jaguar and his followers."

After saying this, the Chimp paused briefly and continued, "It may surprise you to learn, that your earth has been invaded by Demon Jaguar and his henchmen, who are trying to take it over. You know a little about what has happened in South America, which they now call ULSAR, and have some idea of the unusual events that are taking place in the rest of the world. This is the work of Demon Jaguar and his band. If something is not done to stop them, then they will take over the entire world. That will mean the end of human civilisation as---"

He was interrupted by Henry who protested, "I am confused. You are going too fast. First of all who are you, and who is this Demon Jaguar, and where did you come from?"

The Chimp replied, "What I said might have sounded strange and unbelievable, but then my coming out of your computer was equally strange. Wasn't it? You have just got to believe everything I say, no matter how strange it may sound. As I just said, Demon Jaguar is the greatest evil being in the universe. He and his henchmen have always been present in the universe, and cannot be killed by any means. Like them I have existed forever and cannot die. My job is to organise the forces of good against them. I cannot oppose them directly. That is the law of nature. Is this much clear to you?"

Henry hesitated before replying. "What you said is very confusing and unreal. Am I to understand that you and he are both immortals like the Greek gods and goddesses, I have read about in stories? Why can't you oppose him directly? Are you afraid of him? Where were you before you came here?"

"Your questions are good, and you seem to be getting the general picture. Let me answer them one by one. I have no emotions, so I cannot feel fear. I cannot oppose him directly, because that is the law of nature. The universe is much more complex than you think. There are millions of parallel worlds in different dimensions. Your solar system and all of your others stars are repeated millions of times, and there is no way by which your science can detect the existence of these parallel worlds. No heat, light, sound or any form of energy or matter can travel from one world to the other, but there are no such restrictions on Demon Jaguar and his gang, or on me. We can travel freely from one world to the other and go to any planet or star in the blink of an eyelid."

"Wow! That's great. You must travel at the speed of light," Henry interrupted.

"No," replied the Chimp, "we are even faster. At the speed of light, it would take me years to travel from one star to another. I travel with the speed of thought. I decide where I have to go, and I reach that place immediately. Demon Jaguar and his gang can also do the same. Before this I was on another planet, in another world, which had been invaded by Demon Jaguar. The intelligent life there was silicon based. I am glad to say that the beings there defeated Demon Jaguar, with a little bit of help from me. Then he came to your earth, and I came here in search of him."

"Good! Do you always manage to beat Demon Jaguar?" asked Henry. "What took you so long to reach the Earth?"

"These are really good questions. This confirms my opinion that you are a really intelligent boy." replied the Chimp. "Looking for him is almost like looking for a needle in a haystack. Many times I am late in catching up with Demon Jaguar. We are not gods, but you get the picture. Demon Jaguar came to your world about three years ago to take it over. He has already completed the takeover of South America, where people believe he is the new God, and is being worshipped like one but, mark my words, he is the devil. He gains power from the worship of his people. With each passing day the number of his worshippers increase, and his power grows. At the same time their mental capabilities reduce. They will shortly lose interest in music, arts, literature and anything that requires creative ability Soon they will almost reach the mental level of animals. If he takes over the entire world then your civilisation will come to an end. When he has sucked out the intelligence from every human mind, he and his henchmen will travel to some other world, which has intelligent life to repeat what they have done here. This should give you a clear picture of what is in store for your world," saying this, the Chimp waited for Henry's response.

"It is really frightening. Surely there is something you can do about it. Can you not warn the president of America and the governments of other countries?" was all Henry could say.

The Chimp responded, "That will not help. Most governments are in a state of confusion. Some petty politicians, officials and military officers are under the control of Demon Jaguar and his henchmen. Even if your president were to take military action against ULSAR, it would probably be defeated as they have better weapons. A nuclear attack would be a disaster. It might kill almost everyone in ULSAR but will have no physical effect on Demon Jaguar and his bunch. With his supporters gone, he may shift to another world, or simply shift base to Africa where he has a toehold. We can't think of devastating an entire continent and killing so many innocent people just for that. I have a plan to drive him out with the minimum loss of life."

"What's your plan?" was Henry's eager response.

In a calm and clear voice the Chimp replied, "It is my firm opinion that you are the best person to lead the fight against these invaders."

"That's the silliest thing I have heard in all my life. I just can't believe it," protested Henry.

"It may sound crazy, but it is true," replied the Chimp and continued. "Demon Jaguar has an electronics network to keep track of the thoughts of a very large percentage of the adult population of the world. This includes all of the important people in government, the military, business etcetera and random selections of common citizens of all countries. He would come to know what is being planned, and would take suitable action immediately. Hence, children are the best bet. I arrived on your earth about two months ago, as it took me a long time searching for him on so many different planets in millions of worlds. Since then I have done a lot of research, mostly through your computer networks and by other means also. I know you are very brave and have excellent leadership qualities. You also have a group of very brave and loyal friends, who will help you. That's why I have selected you. I will be your guide and guardian angel. I will give good advice and super powers, as and when you need them. However, victory will depend on you and your friends. The fate of the world is at stake. Are you willing to take up the challenge?"

Henry replied, "Oh! I can't say. What chance do my friends and I have against such powerful immortal beings? How do I approach my friends? They are not going to believe me when I tell them about you and Demon Jaguar and his gang. They are definitely not going to swallow any wild tales about alien beings trying to take over the world. At best they will laugh at me. Soon the whole school will be laughing at me for telling such weird tales."

"Calm down! Do have some confidence in yourself and your friends," said the Chimp. "At first they may not believe what you say, but you should make an effort to convince them once. If you fail, tell them to meet me at some secluded place, I will try to convince them that it is all true."

"Ok. I shall talk with them tomorrow and try to arrange a meeting with you," replied Henry, "but I can't promise that they will join the fight."

"Leave that part to me. When you want to contact me, visualise my image in your mind, and repeat my name twice in a gentle whisper, and I will get in touch with you," after saying this, the Chimp bid him good night. Then he went back into the computer screen in the same way as he had come out of it. For a couple of minutes Henry sat thinking about what had happened. Looking at the table clock, he saw that it was past midnight. He set the alarm for 6 am as he was afraid that he might oversleep and miss the school bus. Soon he was in bed and snoring loudly.

❖❖❖

Chapter 3

THE MEETING IN THE TREEHOUSE

Henry's home was about a quarter of a mile from the nearest street, located on an isolated plot, several acres in size. A winding country lane branched off from the street, and passed in front of the driveway, and continued to a lake about half a mile behind the house. Between the house and the lake was a small forest with the clearing in which the children usually played. The forest extended beyond the lake, up to a low range of hills a mile or so behind the lake.

The house itself was double storied, and had a large basement. There was a huge lawn in front with a few fruit trees and a large number of flower beds. Behind the house there was a large open space with a swimming pool and many big trees at the back. One of them had a wooden tree house, built by Henry's father about a year ago with the help of the five friends.

Mr. Taylor was a good amateur carpenter and had made the house for Henry and his friends, because he did not want them to use the basement, which was reserved as his private den. This suited the children well, as they could talk loudly in the tree house without anyone in the house hearing anything at all. Also, the view from the tree was grand. They could see the lake and the forest, a short distance behind the house with hills in the background.

The next morning Henry wasn't quite sure whether the Chimp had visited, or it had all been a dream. Just to make sure he visualized the Chimp in his mind and whispered his name twice. The Chimp appeared, and said, "It wasn't a dream. Good thing you called. Now you have learned how to summon me." Then he vanished from sight.

Having eaten breakfast, Henry and his sister, Joan, were walking towards the main road to board their school bus. He was thinking about how to tell his friends, about the Chimp and his story. Would they believe him, or simply laugh at him? He would have to be careful about what he said, and how he said it. By the time they reached the bus stop he had made up his mind about how to break the story to his friends. Robert and Diego were already in the bus. Henry went and sat on the empty seat next to Robert and whispered to him, "There is something really important as well as top secret that I wanted to talk with you, Diego, Marie and John. Please come to my house today at 4 O' clock sharp. We could talk in the tree house."

"What is it about?" Robert asked in a surprised tone. "It's a long story, can't tell right now," replied Henry, "Please pass on the message to Diego, and I will tell John and Marie." At the next stop he went and sat next to John and passed on the same message to him also. Well before the bus reached school, the other two had also been told.

Shortly before four in the evening, all the friends were at Henry's home enjoying the delicious apple pie, tomato and cheese sandwiches, cookies and fruit juice- all made by Mrs. Taylor. She took pride in whatever she made, and the children were always keen to eat her home made treats. It always made her happy to see the children enjoy her meals. After having eaten till they were full, they thanked her, and went out of the back door. To get into the tree house, they had to climb a steep ladder, as the house itself rested on some branches about twenty feet above the ground. It was past four thirty by the time they were inside the tree house. Marie spoke up, "The suspense is getting on my nerves, so you had better tell what you have to say quickly."

Henry told them about the Chimp's visit and much of what he had said, but left out the parts which were more difficult to believe. At first they were skeptical and he was interrupted several times. Then they allowed him to proceed, but raised questions from time to time. It took about thirty to forty minutes before Henry completed his story. Then he said, "We have to decide whether we take up the fight against Demon Jaguar and his gang. The stakes are very high, and there is considerable danger to our lives. I am not sure if our best efforts, and help from the Chimp, will be enough to defeat the enemy. If anyone of you wants to opt out, you may do so now, or after meeting the Chimp and listening to what he tells us."

At this, there were loud protests from his friends, all of whom gave their immediate consent. Marie said. "We all must try our best. I do not mind getting killed in the struggle to save the world. The very thought that we can fight back has raised my spirits. Delay in starting the fight will help Demon Jaguar get stronger, so let the fight begin today itself." This enthusiastic response was just the right tonic to lift Henry's spirits. That night Henry visualised the Chimp's image and repeated his name twice, and after a short pause asked him, "Do you hear me."

"Yes, I do" replied the Chimp. "Our meeting was much better than I expected. They didn't laugh at me or think that I had gone crazy. At first they had their doubts about the story, but then they all agreed to be part of the team against Demon Jaguar and his gang. In fact, the latest news of the events in Zimbabwe and other parts of Africa has made them so eager to get into action, that they want a meeting with you tomorrow itself. Shall I fill you in with all of the details of our meeting?"

"That won't be necessary. Actually, I had tuned myself into your meeting and so I saw and heard all that happened. It was as good as being present at the meeting and no one being the wiser for it. That was exactly the kind of response I was hoping from your friends."

"That was a really sneaky, invasion of privacy kind of thing. Why didn't you tell me before that you would be eaves dropping on us?"

"Sorry, but with time you will get wise to my ways. If you or your friends had known beforehand that I would be observing your meeting, then you all would not have spoken freely. You can rest assured that I did not use any kind of mind control technique on anyone, because it was essential that you take the decision of your own free will. I am really pleased that you are eager for action."

After a short pause the Chimp continued, "From now on, whenever you are doing anything important or dangerous, I shall be present near you, though you won't be able to see me. Don't let that affect your independent thinking. Do what your mind tells you. By staying close to you I may be able to save you from danger."

"That's good. We have the benefit of your protection, while we are free to use our own judgment. Will you come to our tree house tomorrow at five in the evening to meet my friends?"

"Yes that is fine. I will make my entry after all of you are inside the tree house."

That night Henry dreamt about Demon Jaguar and his gang. At first he saw them talking with each other, but then suddenly they saw him, and rushed towards him. Their faces were scary. The dream turned into a night mare. For a short while, he stood paralysed with fear and then turned and ran. The evil pack chased him. He ran bare footed, in his night clothes, through the forest behind his home. They were getting close. He reached the edge of the lake, and jumped in before they could catch him. That was when he woke up drenched in sweat and breathing fast. The nightmare had seemed so real that it took him a while to recover. Then he thought about the others and wondered if any of them were having night mares. It took him a while to calm down before he could fall asleep again. This time he slept peacefully.

❖❖❖

Chapter 4

THE FRIENDS MEET THE CHIMP

The next day Henry and his friends were eagerly waiting in the tree house for the Chimp to appear. They had feasted on the delicious meal served by Mrs. Taylor. There was excitement in the air. What kind of entry would the Chimp make? That was the question in everyone's mind. Soon a piece of paper floated into the room through the window, and became stationary in a vertical position directly above the table around which everyone had been sitting. Then the drawing on the paper transformed itself gradually into the Chimp. Seeing the expression of wonder and awe on the faces of Henry's friends he said, "Henry, for you, my appearance is a rerun of my first visit, but I wanted to impress your friends and see the expressions of wonder on their faces. They have not let me down."

Marie clapped her hands and said, "You made a wonderful entry. You look pleasant and friendly, and much nicer than any chimpanzee like man that I have seen. Oops, what a stupid remark! I have never even seen a chimpanzee like man before."

"Thank you for the compliment. I do believe that a little bit of showmanship impresses people, particularly if they are young children. Now to complete the formality, let each one of you introduce yourself," said the Chimp.

He continued after the introductions, "Henry told me that you all are willing to fight Demon Jaguar, but are not sure if you can beat him. Right now the odds may not appear to be in your favor, but let us make an analysis of the situation. He has four assistants which adds up to five, and he will get the support of the local evil spirits. I think that you are all outstanding children, and that makes all the difference between winning and losing. I will make sure that you get the support of the local good spirits. In addition, I will give you guidance, and also many magical gifts and powers when the time is right. I will be your coach as well as guardian angel. I cannot involve myself directly in the fight, but still you can count me as the sixth member of your team. Hence you have the numerical advantage, plus you also have the benefit of secrecy on your side.

They won't know anything about you, but you will find out more and more about their activities. If the need arises, we will take the help of some reliable grownups later. Let me make it absolutely clear, that no grownup should come to know anything at all about it, till I decide. Otherwise it may put your whole mission in jeopardy. Demon Jaguar's men scan the thoughts of almost all important grownups in most parts of the world. If any grownup finds out that you are involved in the fight against him, then he may trace you and try to kill you. His agents even check on the emails and tap many phones. I am sure you are sensible children, and will not even let your parents or brothers and sisters know anything about your activities. That will put them and your entire mission at risk."

"Yes we understand," they responded, except Marie who asked, "What about our thoughts. If he can monitor the thoughts of adults, he can monitor the thoughts of children also."

"Not right now. He does not have the resources and manpower for that" explained the Chimp. "Now as I was saying, the advantage is yours, but in any real life situation there is no guarantee of success. Hence you must not leave anything to chance. The final result of this war will depend on your hard work, discipline, individual initiative as well as teamwork. Yours will be a small tight knit team operating in the utmost secrecy. Demon Jaguar has his agents all over America, even in high positions in the government, the army, navy, air force and business. They are everywhere, even in your town. They have their eyes and ears open and report anything suspicious. They also try to win over more people on the side of Demon Jaguar. These are not freemen. They have been possessed by him or his henchmen. His power comes from the adulation and worship of his followers. In South America he has banned all religions except his own. All places of worship are now used only for his worship. Let me show you what I mean."

The Chimp snapped his fingers, and an amazing thing happened. Each of the children felt that they were inside a church, with a large gathering of people and a huge being on the podium. He seemed to be at least ten feet tall with a human face and body, but the hands and feet appeared to be more like the claws of a jaguar. The face, though human, had an evil look, like that of a jaguar eyeing its prey hypnotically. This made the children cower in fright, but to their surprise none in the crowd even glanced at them. The scene lasted only a few seconds, and then they were back in the tree house with the Chimp. "That was a really scary sight," said Henry.

"I took you to one of the churches in Sao Paulo," the Chimp explained. "The giant creature, that you saw, was the living image of Demon Jaguar. The people were his worshipers, but none of them could see you. Now let mc take you to Rio."

'The Chimp clapped his hands and, for a short while, they were again inside another beautifully decorated church with a large group of followers praying in front of the living image of

Demon Jaguar. When they were back in the tree house the Chimp said, "The same scene is being enacted in all of the churches of South America. Demon Jaguar can create as many living images of himself as he likes. Right now it is time for evening prayers in ULSAR. Crowds have gathered in each and every church, and are worshiping in front of his living images. He controls the minds of these people. Each image is drawing power from the minds of these people. These people have no freedom of thought or action. They function according to his commands. In time their minds will lose all ability for independent action and creative thinking. Music, literature, arts, science etcetera will die out. After several generations human beings would be reduced to the level of zombies with little or no power of intelligent thinking. At this stage Demon Jaguar will leave the earth to seek another world with intelligent life."

Marie interrupted, "Really! You mean to say there is intelligent life on other planets? Then why have we not been able to find them and contact them?"

The Chimp replied, "My dear girl, there are many planets in your world which have life. Some of these have intelligent civilised life, different from yours. They are really far away; thousands or even millions of light years away. That's why you have no contact with them." Then he paused for a few second and continued, "I will tell you something which will really take your breath away. There are millions of parallel worlds very similar to yours, and each one of them has an earth inhabited by the same basic life forms that you have here including human beings." This last statement brought out a collective gasp of surprise from everyone except Henry. Marie said, "Now that is something we find difficult to believe. It is really weird that there are so many worlds and we do not even have a clue that they exist."

"Yes. That's true," replied the Chimp. "They all occupy the same space and still they have no interaction whatsoever with each other. No heat, light, sound or matter can escape from one universe to the other. You can say it is a magic trick played by nature. The worlds each have an earth like yours. These millions of earths are similar, but each is at a different stage of evolution. They have human life like yours. Some are much more advanced than you while others are hundreds of thousands of years behind, while many are almost as advanced as your earth." He paused, as if, inviting a question. It was now Diego who spoke up. "How can you say that there are millions of worlds? If nothing can travel from one world to another, how can you travel from one to the other?"

"I said that heat, light, sound and matter cannot travel from one universe to the other, but I am none of these, nor are Demon Jaguar and his gang. You will ask about our bodies. Well these are temporary forms we acquire when we visit an earth which has a human population. When we go to another planet with a different type of intelligent life we acquire that type of body. It is automatic. We have no choice for the type of body we select. Like me, the Demon Jaguar and his henchmen also have no physical existence and easily move between the universes. We are like spirits, but have many special powers. We can move with the speed of thought. If any of us wishes to go to the other end of this world or to any other place on any other world, we can do so immediately. I can't explain how it is done, so let's say it is by magic. You have seen what Demon Jaguar looks like when he visits one of these earths. Let me show you his gang one after the other, and tell you about them."

In the next scene, they saw a very fat man with a small head, short stubby arms and legs and a big belly. "He is in charge of the operations in North America. The one we have to tackle first. Don't underestimate him by his looks. He is very shrewd and cunning and plans the operations. I call him the Big Belly but Demon Jaguar calls him Numero Uno which is Spanish for Number One. He is his right hand man. Now if this person had a choice would he select such an ugly looking body. If I had a choice I would have selected the body of some handsome film star," the Chimp explained. The children understood him and caught the humor of the last two statements. Marie said, "I like they way you are." This pleased the Chimp.

Then he changed the scene to show a man dressed up like a Wicked Don. He had a rather broad ugly face with a broken nose. Looking at him, one would say he was a cross between a Wicked Don and a street mugger. "I call him the Wicked Don. The Demon Jaguar calls him Numero Dos. Right now he is in charge of the operations in Africa. He is very cruel and dangerous and specialises in guerilla warfare."

The third scene showed a tall, slim, distinguished looking man with the face and beard of an intellectual. His eyes were hypnotic. He was in a restaurant talking with two men dressed in pinstriped suits. "I call him the Sly Mesmer, and he is Numero Tres. He is very polished and sophisticated and can hypnotize people and win them over. He is in charge of operations in Europe and Asia and sometimes goes to Australia and New Zealand to initiate action. These two men he is talking with are French Mayors. Possibly he may get control of their minds," the Chimp continued.

Marie interrupted, "I can understand French. Right now they are arguing with him. Maybe later they will fall under his control."

The fourth scene showed the Demon Jaguar talking with a strongly built man with the physique of a bouncer. "That's the Inquisitor, taking instructions from his boss who calls him

Numero Cuarto. He spends most of his time in South America ensuring that people remain loyal to the Demon Jaguar. He is extremely brutal and uses torture to control people. He also visits Australia and New Zealand to help Numero Tres. Now that I have shown all of your enemies are there any questions before we proceed further?" the Chimp asked. There was a brief pause during which the friends all looked towards Henry, as if signaling to him that as their leader he should reply. Taking his cue, Henry said, "We will think and ask questions later. At present we should not waste time. We are all ready for action."

Thc others nodded in agreement. The Chimp said, "Good! I like your attitude. You need a lot of preparation before you get into action. As a start, you have to go on a journey to the past as part of your training. On Friday evening go to the lake behind Henry's house, wearing your swimsuits under your clothes. You have seen the place which has three of the tallest fir trees standing side by side at the lake edge. Stand at the point directly opposite the central tree. You have to jump into the lake one by one and swim away from shore about five yards. Then turn around to face the shore and dive down till you are about six feet under the surface, and then swim towards the shore. You will enter into the mouth of a cave. Swim steadily for about half a minute and rise to the surface and you will be in a pool inside a large and rather long cave with a small narrow stream flowing from the pool. Get out of the pool, and walk along the stream alone till you reach the cave mouth. Wait inside the cave for the others to catch up. Leave the cave only after everyone is accounted for. Then walk towards a large rocky hill visible from there. On the way you will meet some people and the rest will be taken care of by them."

"Why should we all walk alone along the stream?" Marie asked. "You said that we must wait inside the cave mouth till everyone is accounted for. Does that mean that there is a chance that some of us may not reach there?"

"No," the Chimp replied. "It is for some reasons of my own, that I want you to walk along the stream all alone and come out of the cave all together. Please don't ask the reasons. You must obey me unquestioningly."

This seemed a bit odd to the children, but then there was much about the Chimp that was odd – his looks, his style of talking and walking; so they let him have his way, except for Marie who retorted, "You want unquestioning obedience like some sergeant of the marines."

"You have given us a long series of detailed instructions," said Henry. "I am not quite sure that I remember everything. Could you repeat that."

The Chimp raised his right hand, and plucked a piece of paper from thin air. He said, "You are both right. I forgot that you are little children, and I do behave like a sergeant. This paper has all of the instructions. Read them carefully before the trip. Are there anymore questions?"

"What about our food?" asked Robert, "You are sending us on a journey in our swimming trunks only without food."

"Robert, I know about your love for food. Your hosts there will take care of everything," replied the Chimp. "You won't even have to lift a finger." The children found out later, much to their dismay, that this was the literal truth.

❖❖❖

Chapter 5

THE JOURNEY

On Friday evening the friends arrived at the lake and walked along its edge till they reached the three tall fir trees. The lake waters were placid but a bit chilly. They prepared for the dip in the water by taking off their shoes and clothes till they were stripped down to their swimming trunks, which they had been wearing underneath. Henry put on his goggles and the others wished him luck. He took his position on the lake edge directly in front of the central fir tree, and jumped into the chilly water. After swimming a few strokes he turned around to face his friends then lowered his arms, head and shoulders into the water and raised his legs till he was upside down in the water with only his feet sticking out. Then with a powerful action of his arms and feet he sank about six feet into the water. After two minutes Diego followed Henry in exactly the same manner. He was followed by the rest at two minute intervals with Robert to jump in last. It was his task to put their clothes and shoes in a bag, and hide them carefully under a bush a little distance away from the path, so that they would not be found easily by anyone.

After going down six feet, Henry leveled himself and swam towards the lake edge, where the underwater cave was located. When he had first begun swimming underwater towards the lake edge, he was worried that he may not find the underground cave, but then it suddenly became dark, and he was swimming inside the cave. He counted slowly in his mind, till he estimated that half a minute had passed after entering the cave opening, and he was also feeling short of breath. Then he used vigorous strokes to go upwards, and his head emerged from the water, and he gulped the air in rapid breaths.

Soon his eyes got used to the semi darkness around him. He could see that he was in a small lake, inside a long cave. On swimming to the edge, he came out on dry ground. There were a large number of shiny, pointy stalactites of different sizes hanging from the roof and thick stalagmites rising from the ground. A few of these had joined each other to form pillars, which appeared to be holding up the roof of the cave. A small stream was flowing from the lake towards the brighter side of the cave. Henry started walking along this stream towards what appeared to be a distant light, but was actually the cave opening. On his right was the stream which flowed along the cave wall, on his left the cave wall was between ten to fifteen feet away.

After a while it became brighter and he could see some paintings on the cave walls. There was a bison surrounded by several men throwing spears at it. He could not make out the colors, but the picture appeared to be the work of a good artist, as the figures were true to life. Henry had stopped for a brief moment to admire it before proceeding further. Then he came across an even larger painting of an American Indian village with a number of tepees and women and children, with a group of braves dancing in front of them. At that moment he had a strange sensation, that he was a part of the dancing group. This lasted for only a few seconds, and then he was back on the path. It startled him so much that he uttered a sharp cry, and jumped sideways so that his feet landed in the cold waters of the stream.

Then he noticed that he was no longer barefoot, but was wearing leather moccasins and had a tomahawk in his waist band. His hair was also longer, and he had a headband. Startled, he raised his hands to his head and could feel a feather in the headband. Then he realised that this must be one more of the

Chimp's surprises, and continued walking towards the cave entrance. On reaching there he stopped to wait for his friends. By now he had also discovered that his body had also changed. It was apparent that he was inside the body of an American Indian.

Within a few minutes three more arrived. Like Henry they were also in the bodies of Indians braves with painted bodies and faces and feathered head dresses, and Marie was in the body of a pretty young squaw with a single feather in her head band. They were all rather puzzled by their transformations.

"I think it is a bad dream," said John. "I hope I wake up soon."

Henry replied, "No. It is one of the surprises that the Chimp has in store for us. I am sure there are a lot more surprises ahead of us on this trip."

"Oh sure," replied Diego. "We had better be on the lookout for more of them. This one nearly knocked me out cold."

"I agree with you," said Marie. "It's the weirdest experience I have had in all my life. This new body is fine, but I would like to get back into my own as soon as possible."

"Me too," said John. "What will happen if the Chimp cannot get us back into our own bodies? I wonder where they are. I hope nobody else is using mine."

"Don't worry," said Diego reassuringly. "I am sure the Chimp knows what he is doing There must be a good reason why he has done this. I say, since we don't recognize each other in our new bodies let's introduce ourselves so that everyone knows who is who. Henry, you start."

"I am Henry," said Henry, "but from now on you will know me as Brave Lion, the Salamish brave." This last part startled him as well the others.

John said, "You have thought up a nice name to go with your new body."

"I just can't understand why I said that. Maybe it is another one of the Chimp's tricks. Oh! I get it. This is the Chimp's way of telling us the name of the warrior whose body I am occupying. We'll find out as soon as the rest of you introduce yourselves," said Henry. This was confirmed by the responses from the rest of them.

"I am Diego, but for you I.am Red Moon the Salamish brave."

"I don't have to tell you who I am, but you may call me Bright Star the Salamish girl. I nurse the injured braves and if needed I can swing a tomahawk or use a spear or bow and arrows as well as any brave."

"I am John, but for you I am Morning Sun a Salamish brave."

"There are only four of us!" exclaimed Henry. "Robert hasn't come yet. I hope he is alright."

"Maybe, it took him time to find a suitable place to hide our stuff," said John. They waited anxiously for over half an hour. Finally they saw an Indian brave coming at a fast pace. When he came close, he gave a startled cry and turned around as if to run. Henry shouted, "Robert, stop. It is alright. The Chimp has put us in the bodies of Indian braves." Robert halted, turned around and answered with obvious relief, "The shock of seeing strangers almost gave me a heart attack."

"Why did you take so long," asked Henry. "We were terribly worried. We have been waiting for more than half an hour."

"I searched for a suitable hiding place for our bags," replied Robert. "Just when I was about to jump into the lake, an old man showed up suddenly and tried to stop me. He said it was too risky for a little boy, to swim by himself, so he would watch over me."

"Then why didn't you dive in and enter the cave?" asked Marie.

"Because he would have waited a while and raised a hue and cry, that's why," Robert snapped angrily. "I told him to go away as I always swim alone. Then he wanted to know where my shoes and clothes were. I said that I had left them at home. Then he said that I shouldn't do that as the thorns and pebbles would hurt my feet. He wanted to know where I lived, so that he could tell my folks not to let me comc out like this."

"You should have given him a false name and address," Marie said. "That would have got rid of him."

"The idea didn't strike me, because I generally don't tell lies like you do," retorted Robert.

"Nobody calls me a liar. In future just remember, that everything is fair in war," replied Marie in a harsh tone.

"You two can argue it out later," said Henry. "Just let us know how you got rid of him."

"I told him that I had made a mistake and was sorry," replied Robert. "Then I said I was going back home, and walked back a short distance and cleverly hid behind a bush. He thought I had gone home, so he left. When he was out of sight, I hurried to the lake and jumped in to follow you all."

"Good, that was smart thinking," said Henry. Then he told him everyone's new names and asked for his.

Robert replied, "I am Wild Bull, the Salamish brave. I wonder why I thought of this strange name!"

Henry answered, "That's the Chimp's way of telling us the name of the warrior whose body you are using."

With the identifications over and done with, our party of friends proceeded in the direction of the distant rocky hill about which the Chimp had told them. After a short while they all had the strange sensation, that they no longer had any control over the bodies of the Indian Braves and were prisoners inside them. Robert thought bitterly, "The Chimp was right when he said that we won't even have to raise a finger. We won't because we can't. The Salamish are now controlling their bodies."

Then they saw a group of horse mounted warriors riding fast towards them. They appeared to be a group of chiefs led by a medicine man with a bear mask on his face. He raised his right hand and shouted in the Salamish language, "Hurry up. A terrible thing has happened." Surprisingly Henry and his friends understood the language, but could not reply. The response came from Brave Lion and his friends, who started running towards the horsemen.

When the two groups met, the medicine man spoke, "When you five were offering prayers in the holy cave, one of our scouts reported a large herd of bison. All of our chiefs and braves mounted our horses, and followed the trail of the herd. We caught up with it in a few hours, and killed many bison, which we skinned and cut up the meat for smoking. As it was rather late, we spent the night there, and returned to our camp the next afternoon. Here we found, that it had been attacked by the treacherous Wertag warriors. They beat up the old men and killed your father, Rising Sun, because he tried to resist them. They took away many of the squaws and the younger children. The old men say that there were between four and five hundred of them. They warned the old men that we should not follow them to rescue our women and children, as they are too many for us and they would kill us all. We knew that today was the last day of your prayers, and you would come out around this time, so I rode out with the chiefs to tell you about this terrible misfortune."

Brave Lion and his friends, and Henry and his friends, trapped in their bodies were shocked by this news. The former group reacted by cursing the Wertag while the latter being prisoners in their bodies could say or do nothing except feel sad and helpless. After overcoming his initial shock and grief, Brave Lion regained his composure and said, "O medicine man, you and the chiefs must decide how to rescue the women and children. My friends and I will do everything to help in the rescue, but first I must perform the funeral rites of my father."

One of the senior chiefs replied, "We have made arrangements for your father's funeral, and were waiting for you. We have sent some scouts to pick up the trail of the enemy, and follow them secretly, and report to us from time to time. We must not act in haste. The enemy cannot travel fast as they do not have enough horses to carry all of the squaws and children."

Everyone nodded in agreement. After a brief discussion they all agreed that a war council meeting should be held with every warrior present to decide upon a suitable rescue plan. The funeral ceremony for Rising Sun was held in a manner befitting his status as a senior elder and legendary warrior. After it was over the medicine man said, "Today we are all sad and tired and cannot think clearly. Let us hold the meeting tomorrow after the morning meal. Now let us have our dinner and go to sleep. In our dreams we may have a vision to guide us. In the past many of our ancestors were guided by such visions in times of trouble".

❖❖❖

Chapter 6

THE RESCUE PLAN

The next morning the tribe awoke to a cheerless grey sky which aptly reflected their mood. The five friends along with the medicine man and the tribal chiefs and elders assembled at the base of the cliff to decide on a rescue plan. The medicine man and the chiefs all sat on a few stones arranged in a rough semicircle facing the cliff, this being the meeting place for all important tribal meetings. Brave Lion was among them, while the other braves all stood behind them. The medicine man got up and asked loudly, "Did anyone of you have a vision to guide us?" As there was no response, he continued, "I now request our senior chiefs to give us their advice for a rescue attempt."

Several of the senior chiefs took turns to speak, standing at the base of the cliff facing the seated members. They put forth their views with much bitterness borne out of frustration and despair. Their words were very strong, and they talked of exacting harsh revenge, but none could give a sensible rescue plan, which would have a good chance of success against the very large enemy force.

After the chiefs had their say, the medicine man again took his place at the base of the cliff. He praised them for their willingness to take revenge but pointed out the need for an effective plan. He continued, "Among us, we have a brave young warrior who, though young in age has the wisdom which comes from his experiences in his past life. I can say with confidence that he has inherited the fighting spirit, skill and intelligence of his father and our heroes from the past. He is as brave as a lion, and can handle the bow and arrow, the spear and the tomahawk as well as anyone in our tribe. In the recent past we have won several skirmishes with our neighbors because of him and his friends. They have also contributed greatly to our successful bison hunts. My magical powers tell me that he has an excellent rescue plan. I am sure all of you must have guessed his name. I now propose that Brave Lion should come forward and explain his rescue plan. If it is good, then we should allow him to lead the rescue party. This is my suggestion, but it is best that you decide on the leadership issue after listening to him."

There was a murmur of approval from several of the young braves standing behind the chiefs, who all maintained a stony silence. After some hesitation, Brave Lion stood up, and was about to step forward, when he heard a strong voice of dissent. It was the old chief, Black Cloud, the oldest among all of the chiefs. He was a proud man who had led the tribe in combat many times in the past and had made quite a reputation for himself as a fearless warrior and a charismatic leader, but he was long past his prime. His eyesight and powers of hearing had diminished with time.

He addressed the medicine man in an agitated tone, "How can someone so young be the leader on such an important mission? The lives of our squaws and children are at stake. We need a much wiser and experienced leader, and I am the one who is the best for this purpose. I am fearless in battle and strike fear in the hearts of our foes. No one has any doubt about my leadership qualities. You have all heard the poems and songs in praise of my brave deeds."

For a short while there was pin drop silence. None of the other chiefs spoke in his favor, but were hesitant to oppose him because of the respect they had for him. Finally the medicine man stood up and spoke in a conciliatory tone, "O great chief! All here have seen or heard about your past deeds, but what is past cannot be revived. A mere ten years ago you would have been the ideal leader. You still have the fighting spirit and we respect you for it and it inspires us, but your health is a matter of concern. Your eyesight is weak and you cannot see well in the dark. The rescue party will have to ride hard for several days to catch up with the raiders, and your body will just not be able to bear the strain. We will have to attack at night to gain the advantage of surprise since we do not have the advantage of numbers. You will not be able to see well."

After saying this he paused for a few seconds to let his words sink in. The old chief got up and said, "I think what you say is true. It was foolish of me to suggest that I should be the leader. I will remain behind with the old men and children to guard our camp. Let Brave Lion tell us about his rescue plan, and let us all listen to him with an open mind before we decide anything."

Brave Lion took his position at the cliff base, and spoke in a well-modulated and confident voice, "I was hoping for a vision last night, but did not see one. However, I have a plan which I think is inspired by the spirits of our fore fathers. Firstly, we all need to be completely united for the success of our mission. I propose we follow the enemy in two groups – a small advance group which will move fast to keep in touch with the scouts and a second group which will move steadily. The raiders cannot travel fast, because they have the squaws and the children with them. The advance group should be able to catch up with them in a few days, and take up positions for a night attack. Bright

Star will quietly enter their camp, and join the squaws. She will tell them about the rescue, and prepare them to be ready to escape quietly at the right moment at night. She will also carry a pouch of the powdered seeds of the sleeping plant. The women will mix it in the enemy's food."

Then he paused and continued, "After midnight, when the enemy is fast asleep, she should signal to us by giving two hoots of an owl. Then a small group of braves from the first party will steal the enemy horses. This will certainly wake up the enemy, who will run after their horses on foot. At the same time, another group from the first party will make a noisy attack on the enemy from behind, to prevent them from catching up with their horses. The drowsy enemy braves will be quite confused. Some of them will try to defend themselves with whatever weapons they can pick up, while others will run after their horses to try to recapture them. Taking advantage of the confusion, squaws and children will make their escape. At this moment half of our main party must attack the enemy with full force. The other half should protect help the squaws and children and help them mounted on the enemy horses and escape. Once the women and children are safely on their way with an escort, the rest of us must try to kill as many of the enemy as possible. I am not in favor of senseless killing, but it is necessary to kill or wound as many as we can to instill fear, so that they do not attack us in the future. I think my plan is simple and workable. There will be very little risk to our lives and the lives of the squaws and children, if we follow it properly."

He had spoken confidently. This impressed most of the chiefs and the braves. He was about to return to his seat, when Chief Black Cloud motioned to him to remain in place and said, "You make it sound easy, very easy, but my experience has taught me, that we must never under estimate the enemy.

Further, there are many weaknesses in your plan. The biggest weakness is, that if Bright Star is caught, they will torture her to find out our plan, and then everything will fail. Even if she manages to get in, it will be difficult for your group to steal the horses, as these will certainly be guarded. Also even if you are successful so far, it will be difficult to get the squaws away safely. I fear that many of them along with many children will die. Many of our braves will also die. We must be prepared for heavy losses."

Brave Lion replied, "What the great chief says carries much weight. He has raised some doubts. Entry of Bright Star into their group is essential, so that she may explain our plans to the captives so that they may escape at the right time. Also, if she can mix the sleeping potion in the enemy food, it will make our task easier. There is certainly some risk of her being caught, but it is small. However, if she does get caught, she will scream and shout loudly so that our scouts will know about her capture."

He continued, "For this I propose a contingency plan. I will lead an attack on the enemy, with a small group of braves shooting arrows and making a lot of noise. Then we will turn around and flee. A large number of the enemy will give chase. As soon as they do so, the remaining members of the advance group with Morning Sun as the leader will make an attack to free the squaws. At this moment, the second group under the chiefs must split into two halves. One half will attack the pursuers from the rear, and keep them engaged as long as possible. The other half will rush in to help in the rescue of the squaws and children. They will seize as many enemy horses as possible and mount the women and children on them, and ride away to safety. As soon as they ride away, the other group should break up the fight with the main enemy group, and follow behind the escapees to offer them further protection. Good timing and coordination are essential for success of this contingency plan. Personally I think we should be prepared with this second plan, but most likely, we won't need to use it."

Chief Black Cloud said, "Let Bright Star speak for herself. Does she think she can do what is required?"

"Yes I will do whatever is required for the success of the plan. I am willing to give my life for the tribe," was Bright Star's strong reply. Chief Black Cloud nodded his head to signify his approval of the plan.

Another chief spoke. "At night it will be dark. It will be difficult to distinguish between friend and foe. So how do you expect either one of your plans to work?"

Brave Lion answered. "The sky will be lit by the moon for the next few nights. Also this is the dry season, so I do not expect any clouds, and so we will recognize friend and foe. I also propose that our various groups should communicate with each other using animal and bird calls."

After this, there was a long discussion. Some more questions were raised and answered. Finally the original plan, and the contingency plan, were both accepted with some small changes. It was further decided that if the situation changed, the plans may be suitably modified. Chief Wise Beaver was chosen to lead the second group, with Chief Big Wolf as his second in command. The men were divided into two groups, the larger one under chief Wise Beaver and the smaller advance group under Brave Lion. Both groups were again divided into two. Suitable animal and bird calls were decided for various signals.

After the meeting the four group leaders led their chosen men to separate areas to explain the roles assigned to each person. It was only after every man understood his role that they set out for the rescue. Both groups took sufficient food to last ten days. The group led by Brave Lion and Morning Sun consisted of around fifty braves. They started out the same day. The larger group under Chief Wise Beaver and Chief Big Wolf consisted of around one hundred and sixty braves. It was decided that they would start the next day. The old men and children were left behind with Chief Black Cloud remaining behind as their leader.

Chapter 7

THE NIGHT ATTACK

The first group, though riding at a fast pace, took care to follow the tracks of the enemy and the guide marks left by their scouts. By late evening they reached a spring of clear water, and decided to camp there. It was while they were preparing their meal, when a scout came back with news of the enemy. He and the other scouts had been successfully trailing the enemy without raising their suspicion. He spoke, "The enemy has been moving by the side of the Great White River. They do not have sufficient horses to mount all of the squaws, so some of the horses are carrying two squaws and many squaws and their braves are on foot. This has slowed them. Each night they camp by the side of the river. They tie short pieces of rawhide rope to the legs of each squaw so that she can take short steps to walk but cannot run. They do the same with the horses and also use a long rope tied at the ends to two trees and passing above the rawhide pieces used to tie the horses legs. This way the horses can move around at night but not stray away."

"Don't the squaws untie the knots and try to escape", asked Brave Lion.

"They have a large fire burning at night, so anyone trying to escape would be seen easily. At first several used to be on guard at night and the rest slept in a circle around the squaws. Now they have travelled quite far from our camp, and think that we are not following them so they are not so watchful. Possibly, the squaws also do not try to escape as they would not know where to go, and are afraid that they would be killed or tortured if caught trying to escape," replied the scout.

"Do they sleep around the horses and have guards at night?" was the next question raised by Brave Lion.

"There are two braves guarding the horses and five braves around the camp at night. The first night, they were quite alert. Now they have become overconfident, and these guards sleep most of the night," was the answer.

"Good! This will make our task easy. How far are they?" Brave Lion enquired.

"You should be able to catch them in a couple of days," the scout answered. Brave Lion praised the scout for a job well done and added, "The Great White River offers us another advantage."

"What do you mean by that?" enquired Morning Sun who had been listening intently all the while. "Well they won't be expecting anyone to come sneaking from the river. So our horse stealing party must swim in the river to enter the camp from the least expected side. You will lead them along with Red Moon," was the reply from Brave Lion. After this Henry sent the scout back and sent another brave to tell Chief Wise Beaver to move fast so that his group catches up with the first group to finalize the plans for action.

The next morning Brave Lion and his group rode out with renewed enthusiasm. The countryside was mainly grassy with enough bushes and trees to provide cover. As they proceeded further the bushes and trees became more numerous and the land became undulating with low hills and shallow valleys. The next afternoon they met another scout, who told them that the enemy was only a few hours march ahead, and they should move forward carefully. Brave Lion decided to halt there, and wait for Wise Beaver and his party who reached there by late evening.

Brave Lion and his friends sat down for a meeting with Wise Beaver and the other chiefs to make the final adjustments in the rescue plan. Brave Lion presented his proposal. Bright Star would infiltrate the enemy party the next evening, and tell the squaws about the rescue plan. At night she would mix the sleeping potion in the enemy food. Later she would give the go ahead signal to the scouts by two hoots of an owl. After midnight one team of about twenty braves, led by Morning Sun and Red Moon, would enter the enemy camp by swimming in the river and steal the horses. The second team of about thirty braves led by Brave Lion and Wild Bull would make a surprise attack on the enemy camp while the horses were being been stolen. A third team, of fifty braves under Chief Big Wolf, would be waiting outside the camp, to help take away the stolen horses to a point upstream of the camp towards which, the escaping squaws would go. They would help the squaws and children mount the horses and escort them to safety.

The fourth team numbering, around hundred and ten of the most battle hardened warriors, under Chief Wise Beaver, was given the task of attacking the main enemy group just after the squaws attempted their escape. They along with the team under Brave Lion and Wild Bull would try to kill as many of the enemy as possible. According to Brave Lion, the enemy would be without horses and sleepy and confused. Hence it would be easily possible, for the two teams, totaling around one hundred and forty mounted and well-armed warriors, to defeat a force of four or five hundred disorganised and half dazed men on foot.

Chief Wise Beaver liked the plan, and asked Bright Star if she was confident that she would be able to do all that was required of her. Her bold and forthright answer removed all doubts and this was accepted as the final plan.

Next morning Bright Star rode out with one of the scouts. All day they followed the enemy till it was late evening and the enemy halted to set up camp. The men were busy feeding and tying the horses. She sneaked in unnoticed and joined the squaws. The scout rode back to report on her success to Brave Lion and Wise Beaver, who put their men on alert for action if they received the appropriate signal from Bright Star.

A few hours after dark when the enemy camp was asleep, Bright Star gave the signal. The scouts had been watching the camp. They reported the enemy positions to Brave Lion and Chief Wise Beaver. The squaws and the children were sleeping around a tree about fifty feet from the river bank. The enemy braves were sleeping all around them. The horses were tied a short distance downstream near a clump of trees. Two braves guarded the horses four more were patrolling around the sleeping men.

Brave Lion and Chief Wise Beaver positioned their four groups. Morning Sun and Red Moon, his number two and their group left their horses in the charge of Chief Big Wolf's group and walked to a point upstream of the camp and waited at the river bank, ready to swim downstream to steal the enemy horses. Chief Big Wolf and his men took up positions behind some bushes and trees, east of where the horses were tied. They waited in readiness to help Red Moon's group. Brave Lion and his number two, Wild Bull, and their group positioned themselves slightly north of Chief Big Wolf's group. Chief Wise Beaver and his large group positioned themselves further north of Brave Lion's group.

The sleeping potion was taking effect and the enemy guards fell fast asleep. Bright Star gave the signal. The scouts, watching over them, went and informed Brave Lion. His men gave the signal for the start. Hearing the signal, Morning Sun and Red Moon entered the cool water of the Great White River with their team. They floated downstream noiselessly, past the sleeping camp, till they reached a point close to where the horses were tethered. They emerged from the water one by one and crawled along and crept up to the two sleeping guards. It was essential to kill the two guards without making any noise. Two braves covered the mouths of the guards tightly with one hand each, and used their free hand to finish them off with knives. Then they all started cutting the rawhides ropes tied to the horse's legs as quickly as they could. When all the horses were free, each of the braves mounted a horse and started driving the other horses away from the camp. This made quite a bit of noise, which woke up many of the enemy braves who started running after them to catch the horses.

At this very moment, Brave Lion and Wild Bull and their mounted party came charging and showered arrows on the enemy. Chief Big Wolf and his men moved in to help Red Moon's men. Their task was to take the horses to a point up steam where they would pick up the squaws. This was right time for the squaws and children to escape. The men sleeping around them had woken up and had first moved toward the horse. Then they were attacked by Brave Lion's team. Bright Star had already helped the women to cut the ropes tied to their feet. Now she guided them along the river in the upstream direction.

Seeing them run, some of the enemy ran after them, but halted when they saw Chief Wise Beaver and his men charging towards them and showering arrows. The mass of the enemy was caught between the two teams led by Wise Beaver and Brave

Lion. Both teams killed many of the enemy by their arrows or charged them with lances or struck at them with their tomahawks. The enemy, though large in numbers, were on foot and were drowsy, and so could not do much against the horsemen, who made their attacks and darted away swiftly when threatened. In a short while the fight turned into a rout, with the Wertag fleeing in every direction. Some jumped into the river to swim to safety. Others hid in the bushes, while still others simply ran as fast as their legs could carry them. The Salamish did not let up, and chased and killed as many of them as they could. Soon the battle was over. After this they searched the enemy camp for fallen weapons and the enemy food supply which they picked up before heading back to join the party of squaws and their escorts.

Earlier Red Moon, whose shoulder had been grazed by an arrow, and Morning Sun and their team had driven the horses away a short distance from the camp but were finding it difficult to keep them all in one group. At this moment they were met by Chief Big Wolf and his team who came towards them. With about seventy men, it was not difficult to control a herd of over four hundred horses. They now drove the horses in the upstream direction, making a detour around the fighting groups. They helped the squaws and children mount the horses and rode away to safety with them.

It was late afternoon when the two attack parties caught up with the party of squaws and their rescuers. They decided to halt there to treat their wounded and assess their gains and losses. Fortunately none of the Salamish braves had been killed. Over a dozen warriors, including Red Moon and Wild Bull were wounded but not seriously. Their wounds were washed by the squaws who also applied the healing ointment given by the medicine man. Red Moon had a shoulder wound where an enemy arrow had grazed him. Wild Bull had a lance wound in his thigh which was quite painful, but the medicine man assured him that it would certainly heal, though it would take time. Their estimates of the enemy killed ranged from hundred and fifty to two hundred killed and some others were wounded. These men managed to escape with the others. The victors also captured more than four hundred enemy horses and a large number of bows, arrows, lances and tomahawks.

The whole tribe praised Brave Lion for his brilliant plan and then they offered prayers of thanksgiving. He on his part said that it was a team effort, and Bright Star had played a difficult part and credit must be shared with all of the warriors who made the plan a success. After resting and eating a well-deserved meal, they set off for their camp. Everyone was confident that after such a heavy defeat, and loss of so many men, horses and weapons, the Wertag would never again dare to attack them.

In a few days, they reached their camp and the festivities and prayers began in earnest and lasted for two days. On the third day, the medicine man told Brave Lion and his friends that it was time for them to offer prayers in the sacred cave. On hearing this, Henry and his friends understood that this was the cue for them to return to the present. The words of the medicine man brought them great relief. They had been prisoners in the bodies of the American Indian warriors for long. This had been a very unsettling experience. They were also worried about what their parents must be thinking as they had been away for many days.

The next morning the medicine man and the chiefs escorted them to the cave mouth with great pomp and ceremony. The five friends entered the cave alone. They walked along the stream, and passed the wall painting with the dancing scene. At this moment they all felt that they were part of the dance group for a short while, and then were back on the ground again. They knew that they were again back in their own bodies with their swimming trunks on. They all jumped and screamed with joy. Robert in particular, was the happiest of all to discover that his thigh wound had vanished.

❖❖❖

Chapter 8

RETURN TO BENTONVILLE

After the friends emerged from the lake, Marie uttered a despairing wail and said, "Oh, my god! We have been away so long that I am sure my parents must be worried sick."

"Yeah, and mine must be really mad at me. I am sure that they will stop my pocket money for months," exclaimed John.

"Worse still they may have filed a missing children report with the police," said Henry.

"We are in a real big mess," added Robert. "I am sure search parties must have looked high and low for us. The police may have used their dogs to track us. They may have found our clothes in the bushes and suspected that we drowned while swimming in the lake. My mother might be crying her heart out even now."

"That's quite impossible;" said John. "After a few days, drowned bodies float up. Also, if they suspected that we had drowned, then surely they would have brought in divers and even dragged the lake for our bodies. I am sure, that after ruling out drowning, they must have suspected kidnapping and the police may have organised a nationwide manhunt for the kidnappers."

Diego who had been silent till now spoke up sharply, "You guys have too much imagination. Before jumping to all of these hasty conclusions, let us first check if our clothes are still here in the bushes. Robert, you were the last one to enter the lake, and so you must have hidden the clothes."

Even before Diego could finish speaking, Robert dashed off to the bushes and they heard a loud shout from him, "The clothes are here alright."

The presence of the clothes puzzled the children even more. They put them on and were about to go home, when the Chimp appeared from behind the bushes, with a wide grin on his face, and asked in a cheerful voice, "Well, how was your journey? Tell me all about it."

"Oh god! What a time to ask this?" snapped John. "Don't you understand that we have to rush back home because our parents must be extremely worried."

"Yes, that's right, we must all rush home. We have been missing for many days," said Marie placing a lot of emphasis on the words 'many days'.

The four boys chorused, "She's absolutely right, we can't waste any more time here." They were about to rush off when the Chimp spread his arms to bar their way. The children tried to evade him but his arms stretched longer and longer till each arm was more than ten feet in length. The children gasped in astonishment, and halted rather sulkily.

The Chimp said, "You say that you have been away for many days, then an extra half or one hour delay telling me about the journey, should not make much of a difference."

As they had no choice, Henry spoke in a grudging tone, "Alright, I can't speak for the others, but I am willing to give you half an hour, but no more than that. So be quick about it." The Chimp thanked him and said, "Let me tell you something which will bring the smiles back to your faces. Your journey to the past may have lasted many days, but you were away from this world for only an hour and your parents aren't worried about you at all."

"Gosh, but it's impossible," Marie blurted and looked enquiringly towards the Chimp, who replied, "If anyone of you has a wristwatch with the date, you can check out what I just said."

Seeing them shake their heads, he continued, "When you get home, you will know that I am speaking the truth. As to how it happened, let's just say it was by magic. Now, I want each one of you to give me your impressions of the journey. You start first, Henry."

Before Henry could say anything, Marie exclaimed, "You and your silly magic tricks! Why did you not tell us all about this before we started out on the journey? I would have felt much better. It was bad enough being a prisoner inside the body of Bright Star. I could do nothing but observe what was happening. I was really very scared all of the time, while she was in the enemy camp. I kept thinking that if she is caught and killed I will also die. Even later, I was worried whether I would ever get back into my own body or even return to Bentonville. Of course, I also think that Bright Star was a very brave woman. Without her playing her part well, the plan would not have worked out so well. I wish I was more like her."

"You must be prepared for the unexpected. It will make you more self-reliant and give you confidence so that you can handle any situation." replied the Chimp, "You will soon get used to my ways. I don't tell anything more than what is essential."

After this Henry took a deep breath, and said "To start with, I felt very odd inside the body of Brave Lion, with him controlling everything, and I watching like a helpless spectator.

When we were told about his father getting killed, I felt real grief, as if my own father was killed. I was so angry that I felt like throttling some of the enemy, if I could have laid hands on them. It surprised me that he controlled his emotions so well after his initial outburst. His father's death must have come as a shock to him. I think he is a real cool guy. He came up with a very brilliant and effective rescue plan."

Then he paused to think and continued, "During the entire battle, I felt very scared, much more scared than I have ever been in all my life, but I think he was not scared at all. His leadership and tactics were so good, that a small number of Salamish defeated a force of almost five hundred Wertag warriors, without any of their own warriors getting killed. He was very modest about his own role and gave most of the credit to the others. I don't think I can measure up to him."

"Well-spoken Henry. You seem to have observed everything very well and learned a good lesson. You are wrong in saying that he was not afraid. He was also afraid, but did not let his fear paralyse his brain. Instead the fear spurred him into action. I am sure that, when you go into battle against the Demon Jaguar, his bravery and leadership ability will inspire all of you." saying this, the Chimp asked Diego to narrate his experience.

Diego replied, "I was also very uncomfortable throughout. I was almost sure that we would be caught stealing the horses and get killed. Red Moon and his team did a very good job. When the arrow grazed his shoulder I felt the pain very severely. I thought Red Moon would lose control of his horse and fall off. He was without a saddle and reins. Fortunately Brave Lion and his team attacked the enemy at the right moment, which gave us the chance to escape with the horses. After that Big Wolf and his team joined us. Without them we could not have controlled all of those horses."

The Chimp said, "You were in no real danger of getting killed. You must know, I would never have let that happen to you during your training. You are all vital for the battle against the Demon Jaguar. Once the battle starts, I cannot guarantee your safety, but even then I will try my best to ensure that you are not harmed. I am glad that you got a really good scare and felt the pain. Fear is normal. Everyone feels it. Only fools are not afraid. Now Marie do you have anything further to add to what you said earlier."

Marie said, "My experience is a bit like Henry's and Diego's. I was also very scared when I first entered the enemy camp and later when all of us rode back on the stolen horses which did not have the saddles or reins. I kept feeling that we would fall off, but those squaws maintained their hold. Looking back I think the whole plan was simply brilliant. I wasn't at all sure that it would work, but it did work out fine. I think I learned a lot from this experience. Now I feel more confident about taking on Demon Jaguar. Finally, I say, all's well that ends well."

"That was a very good answer. I like your spirit." said the Chimp. Then he turned toward Robert and asked him to tell about his experience. Robert said, "I think I was more scared than the rest of us combined. Riding the horse throughout the battle was scarier than any roller coaster ride I have had. That wound in the thigh was very painfully. I felt like screaming with pain and would probably have passed out, but that did not happen as I was trapped inside Wild Bull. If I remember correctly he just flinched, clenched his teeth and only gave a low groan when he was wounded. He recovered very quickly and killed his attacker with one swift blow of his tomahawk. That was also a frightening sight, seeing a man being killed and feeling that it was my hand that did it. Later when Wild Bull's wound was being cleaned and dressed, I felt terrible pain but he gritted his teeth and hardly made any moaning sound."

He continued, "Brave Lion made a brilliant plan. I think even Alexander the great would have praised his plan. He also played his part very well. I think all played their parts quite well. It was a bit dark, and somewhat difficult to distinguish between friend and foe, but still everything went well. The coordination was terrific. I had thought that the Salamish would have suffered heavy losses with many killed and wounded. Using the sleeping potion was a smart trick, but still I was really surprised that the fight turned out to be so one sided. It just goes to show that when an excellent plan is executed well even a small group can defeat a large enemy. That makes me confident that we can take on Demon Jaguar and his followers."

The Chimp said, "Well spoken! I –," but was interrupted by Robert, "I say, I almost missed the trip. My turn to dive into the lake was last. I hid our stuff under a bush, and was about to dive in, when an old man came along and started pestering me. I had a hard time getting rid of him."

The Chimp said, "You did well." Gave a mischievous smile, and continued, "Guess who was the old man?"

"I bet it was you," answered Marie and gave a big smile.

"Now why did he do that," frowned Robert.

"He was testing your wits," replied Marie, "and you passed."

"That was a low down trick," said Robert, "and all the while we were there I did not get my favorite foods. He played tricks on us so he owes us lots of treats."

"You are welcome anytime," replied the Chimp, "I don't know about the others, but Robert's favorite snacks are cheeseburgers with chocolate ice cream. Anytime you are in the mood go to your favorite place and remember me. I'll come immediately and give you all big treat. But don't expect me to make my usual appearance. I will walk in as the old man."

Then he spoke in a serious voice, "All of you have had the experience of a battle that took place in a parallel world long ago. I am sure it has made you all braver."

"You had said nothing could go from one world to another," said Henry. The Chimp replied, "Please don't be disappointed. It was a virtual trip but I tried to make it as real as possible."

"That's very cool," said Marie, "I am excited that we visited another world. Too bad, I can't boast about it to my folks or to anyone else." The others were just as excited as she was and felt the same way about having to keep it a secret.

The Chimp continued, "Pay careful attention to what I say. You have serious work to do. Please concentrate on getting as much information about the enemy as you can. Try to identify the enemy agents in Bentonville. Identify their followers among the grownups in your town. Use the internet. Hack into their computers and find out about their organisation in the USA, and about their future plans. Make out a good plan of action, but don't start the spy work till I meet you again and approve your plan. I will contact you in a couple of days but if you are ready to start earlier you may contact me." After saying this, the Chimp made his departure in the usual manner, and the children made their way home tired but happy.

❖❖❖

Chapter 9

THE ALIENS REJOICE

Demon Jaguar was basking in the adulation of his worshipers. He was enjoying it and was blissfully unaware of the arrival of the Chimp in the USA, and his meetings with the friends. It goes without saying that he did not have an inkling of their exciting journey into the past. He had no reason to suspect that anything was amiss. Here he was, in full control of the vast expanse of ULSAR and its millions of people. The Inquisitor, whom he called Numero Cuarto, was with him ensuring that the people in South America did not stray from their new religion, whose main focus was on worship of their new god, namely Demon Jaguar.

Many other activities were also going on in South America, all under the direct supervision and control of the Inquisitor. Many factories had been set up for the manufacture of the special components needed for the ray guns. These guns were of several types. The common basic types were meant for use against humans. One of these was like an automatic pistol, another was like a submachine gun and the third was a long range automatic rifle. Depending on their setting these could stun, knock out or kill. The rays could travel through walls or metal armor without damaging them. Only a thick wall or any dense material more than a foot in thickness could stop them. These weapons had proved most effective in defeating the armies of South American countries.

The second type of guns was meant for use against aircraft and satellites flying over South America. The rays could disrupt the electronics and computer systems of aircraft and satellites and also stop the functioning of their cameras and set fire to the fuel. They were long range guns mounted on fast moving autos and were computer controlled. The third type was used against ships or motor boats. These set fire to the diesel and also disrupted the computers and electronics component. These were heavy guns mounted on fast amphibious vehicles, motor launches or hovercraft.

A large team of managers, engineers, technicians and well trained and skilled factory workers were engaged in the manufacture of the ray guns. These guns were being manufactured and smuggled into North America, Europe, Asia, Africa, Australia and New Zealand to arm the followers of Demon Jaguar in these places. The particular component which emitted the rays was intricate and required considerable time to manufacture. Further it was essential for Demon Jaguar to use his magical powers to activate this component; otherwise it would not emit the rays. This took up quite a bit of his time and the rest of the time he was busy extracting mental power from the brains of his worshippers. Both of these tasks gave him great pleasure.

The factory staff led highly privileged lives separate from the common people. They were exempt from the worship and were provided better houses, higher salaries, and other benefits. They were still under the direct control of the Inquisitor. Those who were not needed for any of these skilled tasks had been transferred to the control of the Demon Jaguar for his worship.

Demon Jaguar had also created a vast center for electronics, and computers located in Venezuela. The engineers and computer experts were allotted many different tasks. One group was assigned the task of hacking the computers of important people and organisations all over the world. Another larger group was monitoring the thoughts of important individual in all countries of the world. This was done through sophisticated electronic devices placed in various parts of the world. Here also the main component was activated by Demon Jaguar himself using his magical powers. Each such device could pick up the thoughts of several thousand people within a radius of several miles. These devices had been installed in the capitals of most countries of the world and in most of the cities and towns of the USA, which was being strongly targeted for takeover. It required thousands of workers to analyse the thoughts of so many people and judge whose minds could be most easily possessed. They also checked the thoughts of the possessed to ensure that they were not behaving traitorously.

Another group was involved in propaganda through computers, TV, radio, and newspapers. This covered the full range from blatant praise of the new religion to subtle propaganda through advertisements and faked news written in the world media. Yet another group was responsible for broadcasting rays which weakened the minds and will power of the people, particularly the grownups and the elderly. These rays had only a minor effect on the minds of children but they influenced the birds, animals, trees and plants and created a general atmosphere of gloom. The rays were broadcast from a few places and were picked up by receivers in various places on all continents and rebroadcast to cover a radius of several miles. In this way entire countries were covered.

Demon Jaguar was happy with the manner in which Numero Cuarto managed everything. He was reflecting on what had been achieved during the past three years. After arriving on earth he and his assistants had set up base in the mountains of

Peru. They had worked ceaselessly during the initial few days gaining control over the minds of people, setting up some factories and the nucleus of the electronics warfare organisations. When they were ready they made their first moves, and took over Peru. The other countries of South America fell one after the other. This was the result of good preparation, he reflected. Thankfully, that infernal meddler, the Chimp, had no clue about this. He was probably far away searching for him in vain in some distant planet in some other world. These thoughts heightened his pleasure.

After gaining control of South America, he had sent Numero Uno, the Big Belly, to the USA to initiate action there. Later Numero Dos, the Wicked Don, was sent to Africa to prepare for a take over there, while Numero Tres, the Sly Mesmer, and Numero Cuarto, the Inquisitor, remained behind with him in South America. Later when he was sure of his hold in South America he had sent Numero Tres to Europe with the task of stirring up activities in Europe, Asia, Australia and New Zealand.

Numero Cuarto remained with him in South America, to ensure that his factories and organisations functioned smoothly, and people were kept under control. This enabled Demon Jaguar to concentrate on taking out the energy from the brains of the people, and also activating the special components of his weapons and electronics equipment with his magical powers. The mental energy was collected at the daily prayer sessions in the thousands of temples all over South America. He had created thousands of living images of himself and placed one in each of the churches where the worshipers attended prayers.

Most of the mental power collected by him was transmitted to his four assistants, so that they could carry out their tasks. Right now he was sending the maximum power to Numero Uno in the USA. Also the majority of the ray gun kits and other equipment were being smuggled into North America. He was eagerly waiting the day when the USA would be under his control. After that taking over the rest of North America would then be just a matter of a few days or a couple of weeks at most.

Demon Jaguar knew that Numero Uno was the best for take over operations, while Numero Cuarto was best in exercising effective control over an area already taken over. Once North America was in his hands, he planned to send Numero Uno to Europe and shift Numero Tres to Asia. Then North and South America would both be controlled by Numero Cuarto. The additional energy from North America would greatly help in taking over the rest of the world. These were the happy thoughts that filled his mind. He was also thankful for the absence of the Chimp from the scene of action. Once that infernal meddler reached the Earth there was no knowing what trouble he would stir up. Hence the sooner he and his assistants took over the world the better.

Now it was time for his fortnightly meeting with his assistants. He would tell Numero Uno, Two and Three to step up their activities. He established a link with them, and living images of all four appeared in his presence. He said to Numero Uno, "Give me a detailed account of your progress."

Numero Uno spoke about what had been achieved since their last meeting. The progress had been good and this made Demon Jaguar happy. Without going into details it can be concluded that that Numero Uno had taken over the minds of a large number of people in the cities and towns of the USA and some in Canada, Mexico and most other countries of North America. He had established a strong network in the USA, and was hoping to take over the country in about three months at most and then the rest of North America in another two to three weeks. He ended his report by saying, "After I hand over North America to you and Numero Cuarto, I can zip over to Europe to help Numero Tres. He has too much on his hands and could use my help."

The reports of Numero Dos and Numero Tres were also equally good. The former had succeeded in establishing networks of followers in several countries spread over Africa. He had established his headquarters in Zimbabwe. He was confident of better progress once he received increased supplies of energy, ray guns, and electronic equipment, which was bound to happen as soon as North America was taken over. After that it would be a matter of only a few months for him to capture all of Africa.

Numero Tres was also happy with his progress but said that his task was quite difficult as he had to cover a vast area comprising Europe, Asia, Australia and New Zealand. He emphasized this by saying, "Right now I have too much on my hands, but once Numero Uno comes over we will make faster progress."

All of this had gladdened Demon Jaguar's black heart. He felt that the entire world would be under his direct control within a year provided the Chimp did not show up in the meantime. It was while he was thinking of this gloomy possibility that Numero Uno spoke, "Boss, I have something to add to what I had said earlier."

"Well what is it? Do I need to send you more energy and material supplies?" Demon Jaguar enquired.

"No, what I am getting is reasonable. Lately I have been feeling that the Chimp is somewhere in the USA stirring up trouble," replied Numero Uno.

"Do you have any real evidence of his activities, or is it just your imagination working overtime?" was Demon Jaguar's next question.

"No," replied Numero Uno, "but I am ninety percent sure that the infernal meddler is here. My feelings are very strong."

This came as a rude shock to Demon Jaguar. He spoke in an annoyed tone, "Just when I was feeling happy and on top of the world, you try to upset me for no real reason at all. Tell me about it only if you get positive proof of the presence of that wretch. I don't want any more false alarms. Before coming here we had covered up our tracks so well, that I am quite sure, that the meddling fool must still be searching for us in some far away planet in some other world."

"I agree with the Boss," said Numero Cuarto. "Let us all concentrate on the task at hand. We will take care of that pest as and when he shows up, which is quite unlikely."

"Ok, if you say so. My brain tells me that you are right, but my heart tells me that the Chimp is lurking somewhere in the USA using his devilish mind to lay a trap for us," retorted Numero Uno.

"Then go ahead and listen to your brain and not your heart," said Numero Tres. "This is not the time to let your feelings get the better of you, and get all worked up over nothing. Better forget about the meddling fool, and concentrate on your work and let the rest of us do the same."

There was no further response from Numero Uno. Demon Jaguar said, "Let us end the discussion on a positive note. I am really very happy with the remarkable progress all you all have made. I wish you the best of luck for the tasks ahead of you, and let us rejoice. We will discuss the situation again after a fortnight."

❖❖❖

Chapter 10

THE MAGICAL POWERS

The friends decided to start the serious work of finding out about the enemy network. They met in the tree house the day after returning from the journey. Just before that they had eaten mouth-watering refreshments prepared by Mrs. Taylor. They had gorged themselves on the cupcakes, apple pie, cheese sandwiches and fruit punch. Mrs. Taylor had served enough to feed at least ten children, but it was all gobbled up before her astonished eyes. She offered to make some more but the children were all so full, that they declined with many thanks and words of appreciation for the delicious meal. Robert said, "You are surely the best cook in the whole world." This made her very happy.

While climbing up the ladder to the tree house Robert groaned, "My stomach feels like it is going to burst. I can barely climb the steps."

"Serves you right for being such a greedy pig!" said Marie. "You must have eaten at least a dozen cupcakes. I hope you don't break the ladder."

"A dozen! What rubbish! I think I had only seven," retorted Robert. "I bet you had almost as many as I did."

"No," said Marie. "I have more self-control than you."

"That long journey with nothing to eat for many days had made me awfully hungry," was Robert s excuse.

"The journey seemed to be many days long, but it really lasted only an hour. Besides we all ate the American Indian food. It was different, but was nourishing and tasted good," was Marie's retort.

"You are completely wrong," said Robert. "The trip most definitely did last many days. The Chimp played some magical trick to convert it into one hour of our time, so that our parents are not worried and we don't miss classes. Besides I did not eat anything. It was Wild Bull who did all of the eating, and I was a prisoner inside his body watching him eat, while my own body lay somewhere starving."

Not one to back off from an argument, Marie responded in her French accent, "Even if you are right, you have had three square meals at your home since your return. The dinner last night, the breakfast this morning and lunch today should have been enough to fill your oversized stomach. The Chimp has promised you a treat. As soon as this meeting is over you can go and eat again." The argument may have gone on for some more time, but Henry intervened, "Knock it off, Marie. We have heard enough of your French. Didn't you both hear him say it was a virtual journey?"

"Yes" said John, "now that our stomachs are full, let us concentrate on the important tasks given to us by the Chimp."

"Alright," said Marie "let us go about it in a systematic manner."

"We must first make a list of the people in Bentonville, whom we suspect to have been taken over by Demon Jaguar," said Henry. "After that we have to spy on them by keeping a watch on their homes and offices. We must also collect information by hacking into their computers. That should lead us to other people here and all over the USA and other countries of North America. Any suggestions on how we should start?"

"The obvious suspects are the Mayor and the Chief of police," said Diego, "but there must be others. We should see who among the kids in our school have suddenly changed for the worse during the last few months. Then we can check on their parents."

"Good suggestion," said Henry, "Let us all make a list of such kids." After the list was ready John said, "Let us divide the work. Henry and Robert are computer wizards, so we two should take care of most of the hacking work, while Marie, Diego and John do the normal spying work." This suited everyone. Diego said, "I like it. I always wanted to be a Pinkerton agent or a spy like James Bond. Now I have a great chance to do what I have always dreamt about and also save the world."

"You don't have a license to kill," said Marie, "so don't get carried away and do something silly. Spy work has been glamorised in books and movies, but it is really quite dull and boring work. The last thing we would want is for you to make some stupid mistake, which puts Demon Jaguar and his gang on the alert."

"I can do without your grandmotherly advice," Diego retorted. "Your constant nagging will cramp my style, and I won't be able to work efficiently."

"That's enough from both of you," said Henry. "Let us call the Chimp, and take his advice before we start the actual work."

Everyone agreed to his suggestion, and he called the Chimp in the usual manner by closing his eyes and calling his name twice in his mind. Within a few seconds the Chimp materialised in the tree house. He smiled cheerfully and said, "I am happy that you are starting in an organised manner. I know all about what you have decided and agree with everything. I want that John, Marie and Diego should do all of the spy work in the forms of Morning Sun, Bright Star and Red Moon. That way there is no danger of giving away your true identities. This applies to Henry and Robert also."

John immediately objected, "As prisoners in their bodies, we will not have any freedom of action. Marie added, "To enter into their bodies we will have to jump into the lake and swim into the cave every time. That will be a great bother and a waste of time. It's just not practical. What if we are in a hurry and need to follow someone quickly?"

The Chimp replied, "It won't be like that. You will have complete control. Also to change into their bodies it will be even easier than changing clothes. Marie, close your eyes and repeat Bright Star's name in your mind three times."

Marie did what she was told. The friends were astonished to see her gradually transform into Bright Star, but with a difference that she was in modern clothes. She was wearing a smart blue dress, high heeled shoes, a laptop bag was slung over her shoulder and she held a vanity bag in her hand. Then the Chimp asked John to close his eyes, and repeat Morning Sun's name three times in his mind and he was also similarly transformed. In the same way Diego, Henry and Robert were transformed into Red Moon, Brave Lion and Wild Bull respectively. "Now you see how easy it is." said the Chimp, "and you have complete freedom of thought and action. Just move around and check it out yourself."

There was not much room to walk around inside the tree house, but still the children managed to satisfy themselves that they had full control over their bodies and minds. This made them feel happy and excited. "This is really cool," said Diego.

"Most spies use some sort of disguise, but we have changed our bodies. I bet no spy has been able to do such a thing before."

"That's all very good," said Marie, "but do I introduce myself as Bright Star. People may want to check her id and it won't be wise to use my own name while in this disguise."

"Maybe we should think of some suitable names to go with our disguises," said Henry, "but it will be difficult to get forged identities."

"No need to worry. All of that has been taken care of," said the Chimp. Then he asked Marie to open her vanity bag and see what was inside. The bag contained a drivers license in the name of Jane Kennedy with a Los Angeles address, an employee id card of a popular mail order company, some money in the form of notes and coins, a credit card a folded sheet of paper, some make up items, a pen, pencil, a mobile a diary and a wristwatch. "Wow! You think of everything," exclaimed Marie.

"We have to be careful and thorough in our work, otherwise we cannot hope to beat the forces of evil," said the Chimp. "Your pen has a hidden phone, a microphone and a camera. The pencil is very special. Only we can see what it writes. Even the magical powers of Demon Jaguar and his followers cannot help them read what is written by it. Anything you write in your diaries can be read by us only and will be automatically transferred to all of your computers. The photos on your driver's license and company ID card are photos of actual people with the same name. Marie's id photos match those of Jane Kennedy exactly."

The children looked at Bright Star and the photo and saw the strong resemblance.

Marie asked, "Isn't it very strange that Jane Kennedy and Bright Star look exactly alike? Also how is it that the four pairs of men of our world and another world have exactly matching faces? It must have required a lot of effort for you to find five sets of identical people in two different worlds."

"To tell you the truth, I had slightly modified the faces of Bright Star, Brave Lion and the others to match the faces of Jane Kennedy, Jack Darwin and the others in this world," replied the Chimp.

"Then how is it that the other people of the Salamish tribe did not notice this," was Marie's next question.

"That's because they saw their actual faces, and you saw the modified faces," replied the Chimp.

"Why do you make things so complicated? Why not put us in the bodies of Jane Kennedy, Jack Darwin and the rest of them?" asked Marie.

"No. I don't want to use live people and put them at risk. Bright Star, Brave Lion and the others are long dead. Also, if I use them, their spirits will help you and you will absorb some of their good qualities. That's a big advantage. They were super persons of their time. Now please no further questions, otherwise we won't make any progress. Just remember that you must do what I tell you even if it does not appear to be logical. You must trust me. Now for the last time no further questions. Remember that a team has to follow the instructions of its coach. Is that clear?" said the Chimp with some annoyance is his voice. "Yes, it is clear to us," said Henry.

"One thing is still not clear," said Marie. "You had once said that no matter can be transferred from one world to a parallel world, so how did you manage to bring bodies from another universe. Also how did you manage to send us on a journey to a parallel world."

"These are virtual bodies which I created here," said the Chimp, "but I have imported their spiritual qualities which are not material. Also you forgot that I mentioned earlier that it was a virtual journey."

"It would be easier to understand, if you say that it was all done by magic," replied Marie. "Also magic is more fun."

"Good, now pay attention to what I say and ask questions when I tell you to do so," said the Chimp. "The folded piece of paper contains the personal details of Jane which you, Marie, should read carefully and memorise, but don't destroy or lose the paper just in case you forget something. No one but us can see what is written on it, so it is perfectly safe even if it falls into anyone else's hands. The rest of you also have basically the same things that Marie has got. Now if this is clear then I will proceed further." Marie said, "This is the best ever planning I have come across."

This pleased the Chimp and he continued, "The laptops may look like any other laptops but they are very special because I have used my magical powers to modify them. Firstly only you can use them. They cannot be hacked, so any data you store on them will be secure. You can access the internet directly without any connection. Their batteries will always remain charged. Their memory capacity is virtually infinite and they are faster than any computer in the whole world. You can use them to hack into any computer in this world. Is this clear?"

The children responded positively in awed tones and the Chimp continued, "The laptops will give you any software that you need. This includes all software that exists anywhere in the whole wide world. Now for the best part, if you need to do something for which software does not exist, it will create the software for you if you enter your requirement."

This last statement astonished the five friends so much that they were left speech less. The Chimp could continue without interruption, "Read the instructions for the laptops later, and practice their use before you start your investigations. I want that each one should check that you have all of the items in your kits, and then memorise the personal details of your new ids. I am leaving you alone for fifteen minutes after which I will return and quiz you."

After this the Chimp made his departure in the usual manner. The friends got busy examining their kits and memorising the personal data. Henry and Robert had the new names Jack Darwin and Pedro Diaz, both being computer and software salesmen from Seattle. John and Diego had the new names Wayne Butler and Stanley Garcia, and were computer and software sales men from Seattle like Henry and Robert. By the time the Chimp returned they had even tried out the pen, the pencil and the diary.

The Chimp said, "First let me quiz you on your new ids and then you can ask me whatever questions you want?" Henry, Marie and John gave their new id details correctly but Robert and Diego made some mistakes. "Henry, John and Marie get A grades," said the Chimp. "Robert and Diego, both of you get F grades. I will give you ten more minutes and then quiz you again." After saying this he left and returned after ten minutes. This time both Robert and Diego answered the questions correctly and he said, "That is a lot better. Now you go ahead ask me whatever questions you want."

Henry asked, "What happens if some people here check back on us with our employers, and they say that they have not sent us to Bentonville."

"That is an excellent question. The answer is a bit complicated. Actually I used my magical powers to make Jack,

Pedro, Jane, Wayne and Stan apply online for two weeks' vacation leave, and I also sent them replies from the employers approving the vacations," replied the Chimp. "Later I changed their leave applications into requests for being allowed to go to Bentonville on company business. These have been approved, and the employers think that they are in Bentonville on company business. So relax, there is nothing to worry about."

Marie giggled and said, "Well that is a devilishly cunning trick played by you."

The Chimp also laughed and said, "When dealing with the devil one has to use such tricks." This made them all laugh loudly, but Henry was still not satisfied. He asked, "What happens when these people return from vacations and find that we have been impersonating them?"

"That has also been taken care of," said the Chimp, "When they return they will forget that they had gone on vacation. Instead they will think that they were in Bentonville on company work."

"Oh! That's marvelous," said Diego, "You must be as intelligent as Einstein. No wonder you manage to defeat Demon Jaguar most of the time." The Chimp gave a big smile and said, "Thank you. That's the best compliment I have received in a long time. As for beating Demon Jaguar, that's your job, not mine. I am counting on you to hit him and his gang for home runs out of your world. Now are there any more questions?"

"Everything is perfect, except that we have to remember three different names for each of us," said John.

"That is all part of the spy game," answered the Chimp. "One more thing, when using your new ids, do not think about yourself or your family members as it might give you away. You will be in the bodies of adults and there is a slight possibility that your thoughts might be monitored by Demon Jaguars agents."

"Well, that complicates matters," said John.

"Most spies have multiple aliases and passports," said Diego. "They have to remember a lot. Also they have to be very careful about what they say all the while they are on the job, which may be for years. I don't think it should be too difficult for us to control our thoughts for the short periods we will be inside the bodies of these adult people. Anyway I like the idea of three identities. It feels really great."

This seemed to satisfy John, who said, "I suppose it should not be too difficult to control our thoughts for short periods at a time. I suppose it would be like acting a role in a school play. I have done that many times. Then I forget myself and think only about the character I am playing."

"That's the right spirit", said the Chimp. "Since you are happy with three ids, I will give you the personal data of the heroes from the past. You will find it on the reverse side of the papers with your latest ids. No need to memorise that. Just turn over the page and read what is written. The children checked their pages and saw that the back sides had the personal details from the past. "Right now you must do all of your spy work in Bentonville under your latest names. Keep your wrist watches carefully. I am surprised that no one said anything about them. They too have magical powers I have not told you about. I will do that in the future when the time is right."

"Why do you keep us in suspense like this? Why not tell us about their magical powers right now?" enquired Marie.

"You will be given the powers when you need them and also proved yourself worthy of them," answered the Chimp. "I cannot break the rules laid down by nature. Now go ahead and do your spying carefully. Whenever you need my advice call me without hesitation."

"It seems to me that you simply quote the rules of nature to justify what you say and do," said Marie.

"The laptop, pencil, pen, diary and the wristwatch are great magical gifts," said Diego. "With these in our hands we cannot afford to let you down. Be assured that we shall try our best." The others also assured the Chimp that they would give it their best. Henry summed it up by saying, "We could not have dreamt of getting better magical powers."

"Good luck," said the Chimp and went away in his usual manner.

Henry said, "Now let us go home and learn how to use of our new laptops tonight. If anyone has any difficulty, ask me and I shall try to help. The day after tomorrow, after school Marie, John and Diego can start their spy business in their disguises. I will leave it to you all how to plan it. Robert and I will start the computer hacking work together. Each one of us must enter the daily record of the work in our diaries so that everyone receives all of the details. If no one has anything to add let us call it a day."

"Well it has been an extraordinary day," said Robert. "I don't think there is anything further to be said." The others agreed and they all left for their homes feeling quite excited.

❖❖❖

Chapter 11

DETECTIVE WORK

After his friends left, Henry went to his room and decided to study for his classes till dinner time. He felt that he would concentrate better on understanding the laptop instructions, once the class studies were over. After dinner it took him about half an hour to understand the computer instructions and try out some of the magical features. Then he decided to find out about the company for which Jack Darwin worked. He had just opened the company website, when the fountain pen gave a buszing sound. He pulled the cap off and heard Marie's voice. She had not been able to understand some of the computer instructions. After explaining them to her, Henry enquired, "Well what have you all planned?"

Marie replied, "After leaving your house, we walked together pushing our bikes along, so that we could plan our work. We will visit the Sherriff's office and the Mayor's office and also visit their homes. I will go separately and John and Diego will go together. The Mayor's wife was born in France. I will talk with her in French and get a better response. Diego will try to speak in Spanish with people who have Spanish surnames."

Henry said, "A very good idea. Do look up your company website, and find out what they sell and their procedures. Take print outs of their products, the prices and the order forms needed for placing purchase orders. Understand everything well, so that you can visit the office confidently, otherwise you may make some silly mistakes, and they may suspect you. Keep an eye open for people you think might be under Demon Jaguar's control. Tomorrow, in school, let us watch out for some more kids whose parents need to be checked."

Soon John and Diego also called one after the other. They also had some difficulty in using the magical computers. Henry answered their questions, and gave them the same instructions that he had given to Marie. Then he called Robert to ask about his progress. The latter had learned how to use the computer, and had even downloaded the company material, and so he had nothing to ask.

Henry said, "Good. Now we can start the actual work. Please come over to my house after school, and we shall work together in the tree house. We shall look into the school records to find out the names, addresses, and other details of the parents of the kids on our suspect list. Marie, John and Diego are planning to visit the offices of the Mayor and the Sheriff."

The next afternoon Robert rode on his bike to Henry's home, carrying the magical computer and other accessories. The two boys climbed up to the tree house, and started their work. They hacked into the school computer system, and searched for the names and addresses of the parents of the kids on the suspect list. Henry placed the complete information in one file labeled 'School Suspects', and took a printout. The task took less than an hour. Robert said, "The special software made it easy otherwise we would have spent days, even weeks, over this. I wonder what the others are doing."

"They must be busy. If there is anything really urgent they will contact us", replied Henry. "Now we have to hack into the computers of the people. We have the email ids of only a few of these people. Let's try to get the ids of the rest before we start hacking into their computers. I will enter their names and addresses into some search engine, and see if we get what we want."

After a while, Mrs. Taylor contacted them on the intercom. She said, "Come down soon to eat something as I can't wait long." Robert said to Henry, "Our work is almost done. I am hungry and eager to eat the delicious snacks that your mother makes. So let us go down. After I eat I have to rush home because today we have to go visit a sick aunt. Sorry you will have to finish the work on your own." Soon they reached the kitchen where Mrs. Taylor and Joan were waiting for them with plates full of snacks and milk. They sat around the table, and the two boys attacked the apple pie and tomato and bacon sandwiches with gusto, all the while remarking how delicious they were. Mrs. Taylor said, "I don't know what you were doing up there but it has certainly given you both an appetite."

Robert replied, "We were only working on our computers. Appetite has nothing to do with it. Anything you make is so tasty, that I can eat it even when I am not hungry."

"It's nice to see that both of you like my cooking," said Mrs. Taylor. "Joan is very fussy. She hardly eats anything I make."

"That is because she doesn't eat healthy food," said Henry. "She is addicted to junk food." This brought an angry retort from Joan, "I eat in moderation. I am not a greedy pig like you and Robert."

To stop any further argument between Henry and Joan, Mrs. Taylor asked, "I wonder what you do spending so much time in the tree house sitting in front of your computers. Don't you get bored?"

"No, ma'am," replied Robert. "When we get tired we look out through the back window. The view is magnificent. One day you must climb up and take a look yourself."

"Oh, I am much too afraid of climbing those rickety steps," said Mrs. Taylor.

After the meal, Henry walked up the driveway with Robert. They stood at the gate and he said, "I really need to study for the class test, so tonight I will only complete what we were doing and enter our record in the diary, so that the others know our progress. You must remind them to enter their reports into their diaries, so that we all know everything."

"Right ho!" said Robert. "Now I have to rush off home. See you tomorrow."

After school, Marie had gone home for lunch. She told her mother that she would be spending some time in the Bentonville public library, and return home in the evening. In the library rest room she transformed herself into Jane Kennedy, and walked over to the Mayor's office which was close by. It was an attractive, two story building with a large glass door. She walked in and introduced herself to the receptionist as Jane Kennedy, and handed over her company card and said, "My company deals in many types of goods. We could supply you with all kinds of office equipment, furniture and stationary of the best quality at the lowest prices. I want to meet the Mayor."

The receptionist, a friendly matronly lady, replied, "Oh dear me, the Mayor is awfully busy today, but you can meet Mr. Anderson. He is the building caretaker and deals with all purchases. His office is that one in the far right corner. This is a small town, and our office needs are quite small. You could make bigger sales in big offices in big cities"

"Thank you," said Marie. "Every customer, whether big or small, is equally important for our company. In fact, we have found, that a satisfied customer in a small town recommends us to friends, and this helps our sales," said Marie. "This does not happen in the bigger cities, where we have to spend a lot more effort. We also deal in household goods of all kinds, which you can order from us for your own home. Here is a list with prices. When you place the order, just fill in my code number given on my card. Then you will get two percent off on everything, and I will get bonus points."

The receptionist replied, "I'll give it a try. Now you be careful while meeting Mr. Anderson. He has been awfully grouchy for quite some time now. Earlier he used be very cheerful. Come to think of it, even the Mayor and a few others have changed for the worse. They frown a lot, and are in a bad mood much of the time. I think they are all depressed."

"That's just too bad," said Marie. "I wanted to meet some of the others also, to try to sell them items of home use. Tell me the names of these grouchy people, so that I am careful when I meet them."

The receptionist obliged her by naming four more persons. After completing her work there, Marie went back to the library to transform herself. She went home quite confident that she had identified all those persons in the office whose minds were controlled by Demon Jaguar. Meanwhile, John and Diego had visited the office of the Sherriff, and were able to get reasonable success in their task, even though their method was not as subtle as that of Marie. They impressed upon the staff that their company could supply the latest virus treatment and protection.

Diego spoke with two persons in Spanish and they felt happy and talked freely.

That night they all entered their information in their diaries, so it was available on everyone's computer. The next day Marie visited the Sherriff's office while John and Diego visited the Mayor's office. This way they could check on each other's findings and add to them.

Henry and Robert had been busy on their laptops. They had got the email ids of all of the suspects in the Mayor's office and the Sherriff's office from Marie, John and Diego and most of the ids of the suspect parents by hacking into the school computer system. They spent considerable time hacking into these computers and downloading the files. Later all five met in the tree house, to study the data, which was voluminous. Unfortunately, they did not find anything to link these people with Demon Jaguar or to any kind of conspiracy. It was most baffling as well as frustrating.

Henry said, "We are pretty certain, that these are Demon Jaguar's men, but then how do they communicate with him or with his Numero Uno, the Big Belly, or with each other?"

Marie responded, "Maybe, they use telepathy."

"Not likely," said John. "Demon Jaguar and his henchmen can do that, but these are ordinary people. I don't think he will take the risk of giving such magical powers to so many people."

"I also feel the same way," said Robert. "My hunch is that they have some other method of communication like our magical pens or some such thing."

"They might have magical computers like ours which they keep hidden,'" said Diego.

"That is more likely," said Henry. "I bet their computers do not use the internet otherwise the messages would be intercepted. They might be using some kind of airwaves unknown to our science. The Chimp told us that Demon Jaguar relies on technology far ahead of ours. He has the magical powers to produce it."

"Then let us contact him and get his help," said Diego.

"Not right now," said Henry. "What will the Chimp think if we ask him for help for every little problem? We still have a few days' time to work out the mystery on our own. So let's think and make another effort. Do you have any other suggestions?"

"Maybe if we visited their homes we would find something," suggested Marie. "I could do my door to door sales promotion."

"I agree with you," said Henry. "You go ahead and visit them and keep your eyes and ears open. Meanwhile we will infect their computers with viruses, which no one else can remove. After a day or so we can pay them a visit and offer to help out." All agreed with these last two suggestions. Henry said, "Let us infect all of their office computers, and some of the home computers of the more important suspects. In order to avoid arousing their suspicion let us also infect the computers of some of their office people who are not with Demon Jaguar."

"That is an excellent idea," said Marie. "You do that right now. I will start my work tomorrow. You all wait a day so that these people have time to try and remove the viruses, and find out that they can't do it. The next day, when you visit them, they will welcome you."

The next afternoon, Marie transformed into Jane Kennedy and visited the Mayor's house. It was an imposing house, with a large lawn and several flower beds. She stood at the gate looking at the dish antenna on the sloping roof. Something did not appear to be right. First of all it was larger than the others in the area and it had extra attachments. She took out her magical pen and clicked a picture of the antenna.

Then she walked up the drive way, and rang the doorbell. Soon the Mayor's wife opened the door. Marie addressed her as Mrs. Stuart, and told her in French about the company products and how to order and get a discount. Mrs. Stuart relied that she didn't need anything, but would order later. She said that she was delighted to meet someone who spoke French. Marie then went on her way to visit the homes of some of the other suspects. She noticed that their antennas were of the normal size, but they also looked different from the standard ones, as they had some extra attachments. At each house she photographed the antenna, and made her sales pitch.

Then she went to the Sherriff's house which had a large antenna like the Mayor's but the attachments were different. She photographed it and made the sales pitch to the Sherriff's wife. On her way home she was quite happy and excited. She was certain that the antennas would provide some answers. She wrote about her visits in her diary and also uploaded the photos on the laptop so that the boys would also get the information. After looking at the pictures and reading her report Henry and the others were equally excited.

That evening John received a phone call from the Mayor's office. The man asked, "Are you the guy who came to the Mayor's office bragging that you can get rid of any kind of computer virus. I hope you have the skills to match your bragging."

"Yes, I am," replied John. "Why, do you have a problem?"

"Oh yes! We have a really big one. Our computer system is infected with a virus which our regular service provider couldn't tackle. Even the Mayor's home computer is down," replied the man.

"I will be there late in the afternoon, as I am busy with something else right now," John replied.

Later he received a similar call from the Sheriff's office. He told Henry about the calls. The latter said, "You and I will visit the Mayor's office and home, while Robert and Diego can go over to the Sheriff's office and home."

The next afternoon, Henry and John went to the Mayor's office as Jack Darwin and Wayne Butler. They had a good look at the antenna on the roof, but detected nothing unusual. Even so, they photographed it before entering the building. John introduced Henry to the receptionist as his colleague and said, "He is really good at fixing viruses. He lives in Seattle, and I asked him to come over and help, as I wasn't sure I could to do the job all by myself."

Soon they were in the office with the infected computer system. Henry could have removed the virus straight away, but he spent a lot of time searching the system for suspicious files and was disappointed when he drew a blank. Then he removed the virus, and showed the mayor and his staff that the system was functioning perfectly.

The Mayor was quite pleased and said, "You are really good. Let as have the bill and it will be processed soon. I and a few of my staff have the same problem in our home computers which we use for official work. Please go over to these addresses and sort out the problems and send the bill here. Visit my house first. I will tell my wife that you are coming." Then he handed them the address list. Henry said, "We'll go there right away."

On reaching the Mayor's house, one look at the antenna on the roof, told them that Marie had been right. It was indeed different. They took several photos, and then rang the doorbell. Mrs. Stuart let them in, and took them to the room with the infected computer. It was a desk top with a large memory and high speed, a system which would not normally be found in a home Henry removed the virus and examined the system. He found a drive which he had not detected, when he had hacked into the system earlier. This drive had considerable data in an unknown format. He copied it quickly, and showed Mrs. Stuart that the system had been disinfected. She thanked him and told him to send the bill to the office.

On the way to the other addresses Henry spoke with Robert and Diego who had just left the Sherriff's office after fixing the computer, but otherwise drawing a blank. He said, "We found some secret data in the Mayor's computer. I am sure that you will also get something. Copy whatever secret data you find. We are going to some of the other addresses given by the Mayor. Hopefully we will find something there also. In case you have any difficulty, ring me up and I will guide you."

"Will do," Robert replied. Henry continued, "Tonight I will try to decode the data. You do the same with the data you get."

❖❖❖

Chapter 12

BREAKING THE CODE

That night Henry tried to solve the problem of the unknown format. After considerable effort the magical software could sort it out. The resulting text consisted of alphabet, numbers and special characters arranged in random order and made no sense to him. He was tired and decided to leave the deciphering for the next day. Then he contacted Robert who was still struggling with the format. Henry guided him and it was soon sorted out. The two boys agreed to meet the next evening at Henry's house to do the deciphering.

Next evening Robert came to Henry's house and the two boys went to the tree house. "Let us do the work systematically," said Henry. "First let us compare your texts with mine. "They found that the two texts from the Mayor's and Sheriff's houses were identical and the smaller texts from all of the other houses were also all identical with each other. Henry said, "The smaller texts are probably the instructions for the people lower down while the longer texts are the instructions for the important people like the Mayor and the Sheriff. Probably that's why they are longer."

"Most likely you are right," said Robert. "I think it will be easier for the computer to crack the code if it has a longer message, so let us try the code breaking software on the longer one."

"Yes. I read somewhere that if the message is sufficiently long any code can be deciphered," said Henry. So they set the code breaking software for English and tried it on the longer text and waited with high hopes. Soon a message flashed on the computer. To their disappointment it was 'Code not broken. Try something else.'

"Before we try some other language let the computer try the text in reverse order," said Henry. This also failed. Then they tried Spanish, French, German and various other European languages. When this failed they tried the Asian and African languages and then the dead languages. Each failure made the boys feel more frustrated.

"The Chimp had said that an intelligent person can use the software to crack any code," remarked Henry. "Maybe we are making some silly little mistake. I don't feel like asking the Chimp for help at this stage."

"Me too," said Robert. "I don't want him to think that we are such fools that we cannot even crack the code using the magical software. Probably the mistake is so silly that we shall laugh at ourselves when we discover it."

"We are both tired and are minds need rest," said Henry. "Let us stop. I will tell the others about our failure, and ask them to meet here tomorrow evening. Maybe someone will come up with the right idea."

The next evening they assembled in the tree house. Henry told them about their efforts to break the code. He added, "I am quite sure that we are close to a break through. All we need is the right idea from one of you."

Everyone remained silent. Then Marie spoke, "Let us think about breaking the code later. First let us try to explain why their antennas are different."

"I think I have the right explanation," said Henry. "One of the bigger antennas receives their secret messages from the higher ups, and transmits it to the local followers. I recall that the Chimp had said that Demon Jaguar uses some kind of radio waves to control the minds of grownups and another type to monitor their thoughts. That's what the other big antenna is for. I think the smaller antennas receive the messages, and also the two types of radio waves which whey retransmit so that all areas of the town are covered."

"I think that is a very neat explanation," said Diego. "It covers everything." The others also agreed with him. Marie's face lit up and she said, "I just got a hunch which might help us break the code. I think the larger text contains all of the messages which they have received so far, and the smaller text is only the latest message."

"We can verify that by using the computer to compare the two texts," said Henry. The longer and shorter texts were compared, and the computer found that the shorter one exactly matched the last part of the longer one, proving Marie's hunch to be right." Henry said, "Both Robert and I failed to think of this and thanks to you we may now make the breakthrough." Marie smiled and said, "It was just woman's intuition."

"Three cheers for woman's intuition. Let's have some more of it," said Henry.

"I think they have more than one code, maybe even dozens. The shorter text must be in one code while the longer text must be in several codes if it consists of many messages," replied

Marie. "Probably that's why the software failed when you tried the longer message. I think it should work on the smaller text."

Sure enough the software broke the code and converted the shorter text into a meaningful message in English. Then Henry tried this code on the larger text. Several parts of it were converted into meaningful messages in English while other parts appeared as gibberish. Then he took up the gibberish parts and broke them into smaller parts and could decode them after several trials. They found that four different codes had been used. As soon as the entire text, consisting of about fifty pages, had been decoded everyone cheered. Henry said, "We can read the messages on our computers later tonight. Right now we need a treat. Mother has prepared some tasty snacks for us. Let us go down and eat. Later I will tell the Chimp about our success which we got because of Marie. I will fix a meeting for tomorrow evening."

The next evening the children were inside the tree house eagerly awaiting the arrival of the Chimp. They had read the messages the previous night, and it was decided that Henry would brief the Chimp. Soon the latter made his usual spectacular entrance and said, "From the looks on your faces I can see that you have a lot to tell me."

Henry responded, "We are sure that you know every detail of what we have been doing, but still I will give you our formal report. The Mayor and the Sheriff are the leaders of Demon Jaguars gang in Bentonville. Here is a list of names and addresses of their followers." Saying this he gave two sheets of paper to the Chimp.

The latter held the list in his hand and said, "Excellent work! I don't think that any other group of children in the whole world could have done a better job than this. Let me help you a bit." Names of about a dozen members are missing from your list. Then he handed it back to Henry and said, "If you check the list now you will see that the missing names have been added."

Henry eagerly scanned the list and found that some additional names had been added to the list. He said, "How did you do that? I suppose, It's another one of your magical tricks."

"Actually I had seen your list secretly and decided to help and did some further investigation, and got the extra dozen names," said the Chimp.

Marie added, "I just love your magic. I suspect that you can do everything by yourself. I bet you can even defeat Demon Jaguar without our help."

The Chimp frowned, "Don't you ever say such a thing again. I have explained that I am bound by the laws of nature. I am just a humble servant of the great one who controls nature."

He had spoken with such vehemence that the children were taken aback. Marie's face turned red and she muttered, "Sorry, I have hurt your feelings. So you admit that you are a servant of God." The Chimp nodded his head in agreement.

Then Henry gave his explanation about the unusual antennas. "You are absolutely right," said the chimp. "I have nothing to add to your explanation. My faith in you is justified"

The complement brought smiles on the faces of the children and Henry continued, "We have decoded their secret messages. Demon Jaguar and the Big Belly have selected General William Grant as the leader who will rule the USA after they take over."

The Chimp interrupted, "Let me correct you, General Grant is the brightest and most competent general in the USA.

He is a tough man with an independent mind and a strong character. So far Demon Jaguar and his gang could not take control over his mind, so they have taken control of Mrs. Grant's mind, and it is she who issues the messages. If they fail to take control of his mind, they will drug him so that he becomes dull and manageable. Then he will be installed as the figurehead ruler and real control will be exercised through Mrs. Grant."

"That's most peculiar," commented Marie.

"No. It is quite logical. They need a popular and respected man as the leader, but can't control the chosen person, so they go in for the next best deal. Exercise power through his wife while the people think that it is the man who is leading. Actually General Grant doesn't even suspect anything."

"Then why don't we just tell him about the whole conspiracy," was Marie's question.

"Firstly he may not believe you," answered the Chimp. "Even If he does believe you and starts investigating, the enemy may find out and may eliminate him. It will cause them a minor setback which they will overcome. To win the battle in America you will have to drive out the Big Belly from the USA. However, it is certain that we will need General Grant's help in the future. I shall decide when and how to contact him. It is a good thing that all political leaders are basically strong minded men. Demon Jaguar or his gang cannot take over their minds easily nor can they monitor their thoughts. Otherwise it would be child's play for Demon Jaguar to take over the world. I did not tell this to you earlier because the need did not arise, but now it is necessary for you to know. Now tell me what else did you discover?"

Henry answered, "They have set up a factory for the assembly of their ray guns in California, a short distance away from the Mexican border close to the town of Angel Mount. In a few days a team will drive down from Bentonville to bring the ray guns for their men here. The Big Belly has also planned two major events. One is a fair in a remote part of Montana on the fourth of July. It will be held in a place called Ghostly Hollow. Several thousand local leaders from all over America have been asked to attend. The other is a celebration of Founder's Week, during the last week of July, in which every one of their men is supposed to participate."

"You have discovered their vital secrets," said the Chimp. "What do you plan to do next?"

"We must do something about the factory otherwise pretty soon all of their followers will have the ray guns. Then they could easily take over America," replied Henry.

"It is your job to knock the Big Belly out of America," said the Chimp. "For that you will need to steal some of the guns from the factory. To beat them you have to fight them with their own weapons."

Marie gave him an astonished look and asked, "Can five of us armed with ray guns defeat thousands of his followers armed with similar weapons."

"There is a way to knock the Big Belly out of America," replied the Chimp. "I will tell you later. Right now let's talk about their 'fair' and 'Founder's Week.' At the fair the local leaders from all over America will meet and they will be explained the strategy and tactics to be used in the war to capture America during the 'Founder's Week'. Each and every man and woman will be told about his or her individual task. The Big Belly thinks that he can capture America after a short war, and he has planned it for the last week of July. So you see the 'celebration of Founder's Week' actually means war to capture the USA."

The children looked worried and Henry said, "Then we don't have much time."

"Don't worry," said the Chimp. "We have plenty of time to beat him at his game. When the time comes, we will hit the Big Belly for such a big home run that he will land in ULSAR."

"You are saying this to cheer us up and boost our spirits," said Diego.

"No, my dear boy," retorted the Chimp, "I mean what I say. Have faith in yourself and in me. Think like Brave Lion and his friends. You are no less brave and resourceful than that heroic group."

"Now let me tell you more about Ghostly Hollow," said the Chimp. "It is a private property owned by one of the Big Belly's followers. About a hundred years ago it was known as Sunshine Park. Each year a fair was held which attracted crowds of people from all over Montana, and the nearby states. About seventy years ago, an evil spirit moved in and took control of the valley. It caused many bad things to occur, particularly at the annual fairs. Each year some accidents and deaths would occur. People stopped coming to the fairs, so the owners stopped holding them. The people started calling it Ghostly Hollow and the name has stuck. At Ghostly Hollow we will win the battle for the USA, but first we must arm ourselves with the Demon Jaguar's weapons. This weekend I will take you to the factory to steal their guns. The factory is in a mountain cave on a ranch owned by one of Big Belly's followers. I will give you a virtual tour of the area and the cave."

Suddenly the children found themselves in front of a fence with a gate and guards. A winding country road led towards a ranch house. On the way it forked into two. One road continued towards the ranch house, while the other wound its way up some hills and ended near a cave mouth on the side of a large mountain. Two men stood on guard with ray guns. Inside the cave was a huge cavern with several openings for passages which led to other chambers. Men were busy assembling the guns in some of the chambers. Other chambers had stacks of assembled guns and pistols. Some chambers were the workers living quarters. The inner passages and chambers were well lit, while the huge cavern was dimly lit so that light would not be seen from outside.

When the tour was over, the Chimp said, "I have loaded a more detailed virtual tour on your laptops, and also the floor plan of the cave complex. Please study these and make your plans for the raid on the factory. You must steal about a dozen guns. This Saturday I will take you to the cave mouth for this purpose."

He handed them each a bottle of spray perfume and said, "Use these to knock out the guards at the cave mouth. One sniff of this perfume will make a man unconscious for several hours. Take the guards guns when you go inside the cave. The guns are plastic but have a finish to make them look like metal and wood like real air guns. You will see two knobs on the right side of the telescopic sight. The sliding knob has two setting. Up for single shot and down for automatic fire. The rotating knob has three setting. The first one for stun, the second for knockout and the third for kill. Set the knob on stun because we don't want to knockout or kill anyone. Once inside you will be on your own because I cannot enter. Take care not to get caught, but if you are detected don't hesitate to use the guns. It is most important that you come out of the cave safely with the guns. I will be waiting outside like a guardian angel to bring you back. Let me warn you that the cave has one evil spirit and one good spirit."

"Wouldn't it be better to set the knob on knock out?" enquired Robert.

"If you knock out a man with the ray gun, then the Big Belly will feel a sharp pain, as if someone has driven a pin deep into his flesh. He may become suspicious, and come rushing here and that will ruin our plans. Secondly, when one of his knocked out men regains consciousness, his mind becomes free and there is no way by which the Big Belly can take over his mind again. In a sense the person develops immunity, while at the same time he forgets most of what had happened during the period his mind was under the Big Belly's control. They can't risk letting such a man out of the cave to wonder around in a confused state of mind. They may kill the man or drug and imprison him. These are all innocent men"

"These men are collaborating with Demon Jaguar," said Robert. "How can you possibly say they are innocent?"

"They did not volunteer to join the enemy," countered the Chimp. "Their minds have been taken over and are under the control of the enemy. They are not responsible for their actions, so they are innocent. Once their minds are free they can be rehabilitated to live like normal, law abiding citizens."

"That sounds very complicated," Robert answered, "but I suppose you are right."

"It is. Also you all must understand and remember what I told you just now." replied the Chimp.

"How do you plan to take us to the cave?" asked John.

"You tell your parents that you all have planned to see a late movie on Saturday night," the Chimp replied, "I will meet you in the woods behind Henry's house at nine thirty, and we will travel together at the speed of thought."

"That is great!" Diego exclaimed. "That sounds exiting as well as scary. I hope we don't make loud bangs while breaking through the sound and light barriers."

"Don't be silly," retorted Marie. "There is no such thing as a light barrier, besides no person has ever travelled at even one tenth of the speed of light."

"There won't be any bangs. If you have any further questions you may ask me when we meet on Saturday," said the Chimp and left in his usual manner.

"Let us take the virtual tour, and the floor plans at our homes tonight, and then we can plan the factory raid," said Henry. "I think we should take flash lights and our pens but not much more." After this they all left the tree house for their homes.

❖❖❖

Chapter 13

STEALING THE ALIEN'S WEAPONS

The five friends met the Chimp in the woods behind Henry's house on Saturday night at nine thirty. "So are you ready for action?" asked the Chimp and they replied with an emphatic, "Yes!" Then he enquired about their plan to steal the guns. Henry replied, "After we spray the guards to make them unconscious, John and I will take their guns. Marie will stay at the cave mouth to warn us in case someone comes. The rest of us will creep into the cave carefully. John will stand near the passages leading to the men's living chambers. Robert, Diego and I will sneak into one of the gun storage chambers and knock out any guards who are there."

Then he took out three pieces of rope from his pocket and said, "We will use each rope to tie four guns together and sling them on our backs so that our hands are free. We will come out of the cave as soon as we can."

"Good, your plan is direct and simple," said the Chimp. "Don't forget to set both guns on stun and automatic fire. When we reach there, talk in whispers otherwise the guards may hear us. Now transform yourselves into Jack Darwin, Pedro Diaz etcetera."

After they did what he said, he lengthened his arms to encircle them and said, "Use both hands to hold on to my arms tightly while I count from ten to zero." The instant he said zero they found themselves behind some boulders on a hillside. "Are we actually in California or is it another one of your illusions?" enquired Marie in a barely audible whisper.

"You are a short distance away from the cave mouth," answered the Chimp. "If you peek carefully around these boulders you will see the two guards." It was a bright moonlit night and the friends saw two guards about fifty yards away just outside the cave mouth. "Now I will go and let you do your work," saying this, the Chimp went away.

"We do not have enough cover to creep up on the guards," said Henry. "I will try to draw them here among the boulders, so that we can spray them to make them unconscious. Keep yourselves concealed among the shadows of the boulders." He picked up a few small rocks and threw one against a big boulder. The sound instantly alerted the guards who looked in their direction. One guard spoke up, "Probably it is only an animal hunting for food." After a short while Henry threw another rock. This time one of the guards said, "Brian you remain here while I go over to take a look." Soon he was among the boulders looking around. Henry emerged swiftly from the shadow of a boulder and sprayed a liberal dose of perfume on his face. The man fell on the ground with a loud thud. The other guard called out, "You ok Walter? I hope the fall didn't hurt."

By this time Henry had picked up the fallen man's gun and set it on stun. He peered around the boulders, took aim and fired at Brian, who fell stunned to the ground. Henry raced up to him and sprayed the perfume on his face making him unconscious. The others ran towards him, and John picked up the second gun. Marie took her position outside the cave mouth and the rest crept inside silently.

They moved forward cautiously on tiptoe till their eyes were accustomed to the dim light, and John went and stood guard near the entrances to the men's living chambers. Henry, Robert and Diego tiptoed into one of the gun storage chambers which were at the furthest end of the cave. They saw one guard dozing on one of the crates. Henry sprayed the perfume on his face, and he lay still on the crate. Robert opened another crate, and they took out four guns each and tied them with the ropes and slung them on their backs. There was a smaller crate which contained the pistols. They pocketed some of these also.

Meanwhile the evil spirit of the cave had sensed the intruders. It went to the worker's living quarters and switched on the alarm which made a shrill wailing sound. Henry, Robert and Diego froze in their tracks in surprise. The good spirit of the cave rushed up to them and shouted, "Run out as fast as you can." The three bolted out of the chamber with the guns slung on their backs and made a dash for the cave mouth. By this time the workers were rushing out of their chambers, and John was firing at them. He shouted, "I will cover you. Make sure you get away with the guns."

Robert and Diego raced outside the cave, but Henry halted at the entrance, and turned to help John. He fired several bursts at the men, who were attacking John, and many of them fell in heaps, but many more came rushing out of the chambers, some with guns firing. John was hit and he fell to the ground. Before Henry could react, the good spirit came in front of him and shielded him from the rays fired at him and shouted, "Get out immediately," and pushed him out of the cave mouth. The Chimp was standing there and Henry screamed at him, "Save John, he has been shot."

"I cannot enter that cave, and I must save the rest of you," said the Chimp and extended his arms to encircle all four of them in a bear hug grip. The next instant they found themselves in the woods behind Henry's house.

Marie sobbed and wailed, "Poor John, they must have killed him." The Chimp responded, "Bright Star was a brave woman. She would never have sobbed like this." Marie sobbed even louder and shouted, "You heartless beast. You are responsible for his death." Henry, Robert and Diego felt equally sad, but held back their tears. Henry said, "As the leader, John's safety was my responsibility. First the good spirit pushed me out of the cave, next you brought us all here robbing me of the chance of trying to rescue John. It would have been far better to risk my own life trying to save his. Right now I feel disgusted with myself."

The Chimp replied, "All of you were at risk, and I am happy that I managed to save four of you. I know that you were willing to risk your own life to save John, but that would have been disastrous. Without you four we cannot save the world."

Then he pointed towards a clump of bushes and continued, "Look, someone is there behind those bushes." The bushes parted, and before the astonished eyes of the children, John came out in his own form holding a ray gun. He had a puzzled expression on his face. The four friends ran up to him and took turns hugging him. Marie said, "Thank god, you are safe."

"I was in the cave fighting off hordes of Demon Jaguar's men, when I felt a sharp pain," John spoke. "I suppose someone shot me with a ray gun. I fell and became unconscious. When I regained my senses I found myself behind these bushes in my own body. Then I heard you all talking and came over. I suppose I have to thank the Chimp for rescuing me."

The Chimp chuckled mischievously and Marie said, "You are a lovable guardian angel."

The Chimp responded, "Thank you. Within a couple of minutes you have transformed me from a 'heartless beast' to a 'lovable guardian angel'. You all have done very well tonight. You even managed to steal fourteen guns and some pistols. That's much more than I expected."

Then he pointed to a hollow tree trunk. "Let's hide the guns inside this hollow tree trunk, but first let us take out the batteries from the unused guns and pistols. Please charge them at your homes. Each takes about an hour to charge and can shoot thousands of times once it is fully charged. It is late now, and you must be tired, so go home and sleep. We will meet tomorrow in the tree house at three o'clock in the afternoon."

❖❖❖

Chapter 14

THE FRIENDS LEARN HOW TO FLY

The next day the Chimp said, "I hope you all are rested and have recovered your nerves after yesterdays adventure." The friends responded in the affirmative and Marie said, "I had become very upset when I thought that John had been killed, but now I think it was a jolly good adventure, and the best part is that we managed to get more guns than you had asked for." Henry asked, "What about the virtual body, which John was using and is now in the hands of Demon Jaguar's men?"

The Chimp replied, "When they shot John, he was knocked out and not killed. I immediately sent him back into his body and left the virtual body behind in order to confuse them. The Big Belly rushed to the cave and reported the happenings to Demon Jaguar. I will show you the important parts of their video conference."

The Chimp gestured with his hand. The children immediately saw the Big Belly in conference with the Demon Jaguar. The former spoke, "We caught one of the intruders, who stole some guns from the factory. I wanted to interrogate him but he was dead when I reached there."

"Your men should not have set their guns on kill," said the Demon Jaguar sharply.

"No Boss, they were all set on knock out," replied the Big Belly, "but that meddling Chimp has played a dirty trick on us. I examined the body and it is of a man born six thousand years ago and that too in another world."

"What rubbish! He can't bring a body from another world," the Demon Jaguar scolded him. "Send it over to me, and I shall examine it."

"Sorry boss, that thieving scoundrel made the body disappear," the Big Belly wailed.

"This time that miserable wretch has played a really low down, cheap trick on us," said the Demon Jaguar. "It must have been a virtual body. You must increase the security at the factory, but don't let the loss of a few guns disturb our schedule for conquering America. I will ask Numero Tres to come over to help you out. You concentrate on your work and let him take care of security, and also he can try to trace those guns and the men who raided the factory. I will ask Numero Cuarto to speed up the delivery of guns to you and also send more energy for your use. You were right when you said that the Chimp has landed in America, but we will beat him."

"Thank you Boss. That will be good," the Big Belly responded. "More energy and guns will help our cause."

Then the images faded away, and Henry spoke, "If Numero Tres comes over to America it will make things difficult for us. He might be able to find the guns and identify us."

"That's impossible. I have already used my magic to make the guns untraceable," said the Chimp. "Now that you have the guns, I will give you some magical powers, which will help you in the fight against Demon Jaguar. I have already fixed the guns so that you will have those powers as long as you hold the guns in your hands."

"That is wonderful," said Marie. "Quick, tell us about the magical powers. I am just dying to know."

"While holding these guns you will be able to fly like eagles, provided you wear the magical wrist watches that I gave you," said the Chimp. "You must wind the watch knob in a counterclockwise direction. Once you wind it completely you can fly for around two or more hours. When you sense that you are losing power, you must rewind the knob. However I cannot give you the power of invisibility, but when you are flying you will look like an eagle to anyone watching you, and your gun will not be visible to them. As soon as you touch the ground, you will again look like yourselves."

"Fantastic!" said Marie. "We could not have asked for better magical powers. You keep surprising us all of the time."

"That is not all," said the Chimp. "While holding the guns, you will have immunity against the rays which won't stun, knock out or kill you, but you will feel the pain when you are shot. The pain will be as bad as being shot by an air gun. Don't ever drop the gun, because then you will lose the magical powers."

"Does it mean that, if I let go of the gun while flying, I will not be able to fly?" asked Henry.

"You will drop to the ground like a stone," replied the Chimp. "Also when you are not holding the gun you will not have any immunity against the rays. Don't forget that the watch has to be worn. It is the combination of the gun and the watch which gives you these powers."

"We will certainly not forget this as our lives depend on it," responded Henry.

"Now we will pick up six guns from the hiding place," said the Chimp, "After that I will take you to a deserted area in Arizona, where I will give you flying lessons and combat practice."

"Soon they were in a desert, where there was no one in sight for miles around. It was rather hot. The Chimp said, "If you look at any man through the telescopic sight, and see an orange colored aura around him, it means that he is one of Big Belly's men. If you see a yellow aura it is one of the Sly Mesmer's men. That is how they differentiate between friend and foe. A red aura means one of the Wicked Don's men. In the USA you will spot orange auras only, but will see the red ones in Africa and yellow in Europe, Asia and Australasia. The Inquisitor's men have blue auras while the Demon Jaguar's men have purple auras.""

"It means that we should shoot only at those people who have auras," said Robert.

"That's right," responded the Chimp. "Now as far as flying is concerned, you hold the gun in both hands in the normal horizontal position, and take a few running steps and launch yourself in the air. After that you control your flying with your mind and the gun. You can fly faster or slow down by wishing in your mind. To turn left, and turn right, dive or zoom up you must point the barrel in that direction. However you will need some practice before you become perfect and are able to shoot accurately while flying."

"What happens if someone spots us flying around here?" asked Robert.

"My dear boy, firstly the nearest human is more than a hundred miles away, and secondly if some helicopter or airplane comes here, the people will only see eagles flying around, so there is nothing to worry about," answered the Chimp. "You may now take half an hour to an hour to practice flying and perfect all of the maneuvers."

The friends took running starts to launch themselves, and were flying in an ungainly manner. At first it was difficult to exercise proper control, but after a while they got better and could fly pretty much as they wished. All this while, the Chimp watched them keenly and gave advice to each one, particularly on diving, turning sharply and landing smoothly. After a while, he told them to stop and get ready for ground combat practice.

He said, "I will go a hundred yards away from you, and you start shooting at me. I will, duck, crawl, run in a zigzag manner and also shoot at you at the same time. You must also dodge when I shoot. Let us see whether you can score more hits than me. Each time you are hit it will pain a lot, because I will set my gun on knockout. You have immunity so you will not be knocked out, but it will pain a lot. Don't drop your guns. We will stop the contest after five minutes."

After five minutes of shooting and dodging, the Chimp won the contest by a handsome margin. He asked, "I hope I did not hurt you much."

The children all said that the pain was quite severe. Robert complained the most as he had been shot almost a dozen times. "Are you ready for another five minute session," asked the Chimp. "This time I will set my gun on stun, so it will hurt less when you are hit."

The friends score was much better in the second session and the Chimp was satisfied. He said, "You are learning fast. Now let us practice aerial combat for five minutes. You will be flying, and I will be on the ground."

Within five minutes the Chimp had shot each child so many times, that the pain forced them to come down. "You need to spread out more, and watch me more keenly. As soon as I aim the gun at one of you, that person should take evasive action. Diving and turning away to one side is the best evasive action." The friends followed his advice and outscored him in the second session.

"You are excellent learners," said the Chimp. "Still you need more practice. In an actual battle there may be hundreds or even thousands of guns shooting at you. In future we will have some sessions in which each one of you takes turns against the rest of us combined, and we will sct the guns on knock out and automatic fire. Then it will be difficult to avoid getting shot. Now what should be our next step?"

"I am worried about the Sly Mesmer," said Henry. "He and the Big Belly combined would be difficult for us to handle."

"You are right," said the Chimp. "We must plan a diversion. If we make a few attacks on Africa, that will shift their attention and they will send the Sly Mesmer to help the Wicked Don in Africa. Next Saturday and Sunday I will take you to Africa to hunt down a few of Numero Duo's men. Before that you must use your magical computers to check the internet traffic within Africa. Decode their messages and locate their computers. You will know how many men are controlled by the Wicked Don in different countries and their locations. We will make the attacks where he has the most men."

❖❖❖

Chapter 15

DECEIVING THE ENEMY

Henry and Robert spent the next few days hacking into the internet traffic within Africa, and found out almost all that the Chimp had asked for. On Saturday the friends and the Chimp met in the tree house. Henry told them about what Robert and he had found out. He said, "Their main concentrations are in South Africa, Zimbabwe, Egypt and Morocco. The Wicked Don has anywhere between three to four thousand followers in each of these countries, and maybe about a thousand to two thousand in each of the nearby countries."

"I see," said the Chimp. "That means he has started from the corners, and is spreading his network over the continent. So where do you want to start the attack."

"Let us start with South Africa," replied Henry. "There is a military base near Capetown, where he has a very large number of followers among the soldiers and officers. They visit the nearby beach on the weekends, and should be an easy target while sunning there."

"I would like to see the pyramids and the Sphinx, and so I think we should attack in Egypt first," interjected Marie.

"We are in a warlike situation," retorted Diego. "So let us not convert this into a picnic."

"Oh! That's okay," said the Chimp. "I think it is alright to combine business with pleasure. After we attack in South Africa we can zip off to the pyramids and relax there for half an hour or so and see the sights. In the meantime let the Wicked Don worry about when or where the next attack will take place. That will strain his nerves a bit."

"He has a big concentration of followers in the military base near Cairo." said Henry. "Most of them would be visiting Cairo over the weekend. We should be able to spot them in the bazaars. Later we can zip to Morocco and attack there. Raiding three different places in the three corners of Africa on the same day will send the signal that Africa will be our main target."

"Yes, added Marie, and that short break at the pyramids won't do us any harm. It has always been my great desire to see them."

"I suppose after the attack on Morocco you would like to be rewarded with a visit to the Taj Mahal also," said John with considerable sarcasm. The Chimp surprised everyone by saying, "If you all do a good job today, I see no harm in taking you to see the Taj, but we must start early and I will adjust the time. By the time we finish our business in Morocco, it will be dark in India and there will be a full moon. It is a special treat to see the Taj by the moonlight. Very few people get to see that special sight."

"This is going to be the most wonderful day of my life," exclaimed Marie. "Just imagine that we will see the pyramids, the Sphinx and the Taj, all in one day."

"That's going to happen only if we do a good job," cautioned John. "So don't slip up and make any silly mistake."

"Don't you think we will reach home rather late, if we visit the Taj also?" enquired Henry.

"Yes, I suppose you all would like to spend a bit of time at the Taj." the Chimp replied. "Then it is settled that we first visit

South Africa, then Egypt followed by Morocco, and then India to see the Taj. While you are seeing the sights at the pyramids and the Taj Mahal, leave your guns with me. Also, just blend in with the tourists, and don't get into any sort of trouble as you are not carrying passports."

"We are ready and eager to set off," said Henry. The Chimp took them to the hollow tree trunk, to get their guns, which they set on 'knock out', and in an instant the Chimp transferred them to a place near a clump of trees near a beach outside Capetown. The beach had a large number of sunbathers, and some people swimming in the water. The Chimp cautioned them, "Take your time in identifying the enemy. Don't shoot the wrong people and for heaven's sake don't shoot any swimmer. We don't want anyone to drown."

The friends used the telescopic sights to identify the enemy. This was quite easy as they could make out the red auras surrounding the Wicked Don's men. They counted over twenty of his men and some women also. The Chimp said, "Marie you shoot the women. Henry will take the five men on the extreme left. John you take five to their right. Diego you take the next five, and Robert you take the remaining ones on the extreme right. This way you all won't end up shooting the same people. Now I will count to three and you all can start shooting. Even if we hit half of our targets we will keep the Wicked Don writhing in agony for five to ten minutes. That should give us plenty of time to make our getaway to the pyramids in Egypt before he reaches this place."

The children started shooting and their targets started slumping on the beach. Within a couple of minutes they had got almost all of their targets. At first the rest of the crowd did not understand what was happening, and then there was a sudden buzz, followed by panic and commotion with some people trying to revive those who had fallen, and summoning the life guards for help, while the majority ran away as fast as they could. The Chimp encircled the five friends in his arms, and transported them to a place near the pyramids, behind a small mound. He said, "That was good shooting. You got over twenty of his people. They will recover after thirty to forty minutes and will have forgotten much about the Wicked Don and the Demon Jaguar, and the good part is that he cannot regain control over their minds as they have developed immunity. That was an exclusive beach, and most of those men ranked quite high in his network, so you have caused him a big loss. Right now he is in so much pain that he cannot do anything, but will be furious when he reaches there, and finds out the damage that you have caused. A couple of his men escaped and they will give him the report, but they have no real clue as to how it happened. He will get in touch with Demon Jaguar immediately, but will not be able to tell him much. Now you will see what happened to him."

He showed them a short sequence of the Wicked Don. First he was hopping around screaming at the top of his voice, and then he fell and rolled around on the ground writhing in agony. The children couldn't help laughing till their stomachs ached. "Let me guess," said Henry. "He was hopping around and screaming while we were shooting his men. When he could not bear the pain he fell on the ground and rolled in agony."

"You are absolutely right, and if you could shoot a few thousand of his men in a short time he will be knocked out. His unconscious body will fly off to the Demon Jaguar in South America." said the Chimp.

Henry became excited and asked, "Why don't we try to do that?"

"We could do that if a few thousand of his followers were assembled in one place, but that is not so," replied the Chimp. "After you shot his followers it took time for him to recover from the pain and he went to the beach to investigate. Then he spoke with Demon Jaguar and told him he had lost two dozen of his men including three from among the topmost leaders in South Africa. Demon Jaguar told him to find replacements quickly and to drug the freed men and hold them as prisoners in some secret location."

"That's too bad! I feel sorry for those men and women," said Marie.

"It could have been much worse. He could have ordered the Wicked Don to kill them," replied the Chimp. "Now I will take your guns, and you go to the pyramids and mingle with the tourists and enjoy the sights."

The children spent a most interesting hour viewing the pyramids and the Sphinx. There were a large number of tourists from all over the world. There was a tour group with a guide. The five friends tagged along behind this group. The guide had a deep voice with an Egyptian accent which sounded interesting to the children. He told many anecdotes about the pyramid and the Sphinx. Later they walked towards the prearranged spot to meet the Chimp. Marie said, "Thanks! That was really interesting. I wish I could have spent more time here. Now I am excited about going to Agra to see the Taj Mahal."

"Maybe you should save the Taj visit for your honeymoon," said Diego cheekily, in his Spanish accent.

"I will certainly visit it again on my honeymoon," retorted Marie in her French accent. "Don't let it bother you, because I won't be going with you."

"Shut up both of you!" said Henry. "Let's concentrate on the next attack. We have to use different tactics in Cairo. I think we should land on the roof of a high building near a market square. Then we can spot a few more of his men in the crowd there. This time we will have to be even more careful that we don't shoot the wrong people, as they will all be moving around close together."

"I will take you to such a place," said the Chimp. "If there are more than a dozen of his men there, you can start shooting after each one of you has chosen his targets."

They zipped off and landed on the roof of a tall building in Cairo. In front of the building there was a market square teaming with people, behind was a park with people sitting on the benches and lawns and strolling on the paths. The children unscrewed their telescopic sights from the guns, and peered carefully over the parapet walls to sight their victims. Marie and Robert scanned the park and identified about a dozen people with the flaming red auras while the others identified over two dozen in the market place. The targets were agreed upon. They put the sights back on the guns, and started shooting at the signal from Henry. In about two or three minutes the shooting was over, and they had shot over twenty people.

By now there was pandemonium in the market place and the park, with most people trying to flee wildly. The Chimp quickly encircled the friends in his arm, and flew off to Morocco and landed on top of a tall building near a bazaar. Again they identified the enemy, and shot a large number before flying off to Agra to see the Taj Mahal.

The Chimp let them spend over an hour there. The moon was shining bright and the Taj looked very different from the daytime pictures which they had seen. They mingled with the tourists and walked along the garden paths and enjoyed every minute of it. There were a large number of tourists including many Indians in their different dresses. The children particularly admired the ladies in their colorful dresses. Marie did not feel like leaving, and had to be persuaded to leave. The Chimp took them back to Bentonville behind the clump of bushes, and they hid their guns in the hollow tree.

Marie gushed, "Such an eventful day, and what wonderful sights and I can't even brag about it to anyone." Diego said, "Let us get rid of the Demon Jaguar first, then you can brag to your heart's content. Later when you become a granny, you can tell the story to all of your grandchildren." The rest roared with laughter, and Marie retorted in her French accent, "I suppose you all won't tell the story to your grandchildren, because you will keep it a secret even then."

The Chimp said, "You did a wonderful job. You got well over fifty of his men including about a half a dozen of the topmost leaders. That creates a big gap in his team which will be difficult to fill. The best part is that you have created a lot of doubts in the minds of the enemy. Now they are not sure whether we intend to attack in America or in Africa. A few more attacks in Africa, and they will believe that it is the next target."

Henry had a thoughtful look in his eyes. He said, "Tomorrow they will be alert and we will not get such easy targets. I am sure that the Wicked Don will order his men not to go to public places in large numbers. We will probably have to catch his men in their homes or in their military bases or in the markets."

"You are right," said the Chimp. "Plan your attacks accordingly."

"Tonight Robert and I will try to locate those groups of enemy homes which are close to each other," said Henry. "You could leave us at a nearby place, and each one of us could fly to separate houses and coordinate our attacks by using our communication pen radios."

"I suppose you expect them to be waiting outside their homes to give us easy targets," said Marie.

"Tomorrow is a Sunday," said Henry. "There is a possibility that some of them may be working in their gardens. Some of those who are inside may be visible through the windows. We will make an attack only if we are sure of getting at least three of the enemy, and then fly back to the Chimp to go off to a new place before the Wicked Don recovers. Of course we may draw a blank at a few places."

"Flying over the military bases and shooting people there may be a bit risky," said Diego. "What if they are armed and start shooting back?"

"Only a few of the soldiers are likely to be the enemy," answered the Chimp, "and you will shoot them. Even if the others notice you, they will see you only as eagles flying. Even if a few of the enemy survive they won't link the attack to unarmed eagles, but will be most puzzled when they see that the men knocked out don't even have a scratch on their bodies. So our secret of you all flying as eagles will remain safe from the Wicked Don and his men. That's what matters."

"You can also fly over the markets as eagles and shoot up the enemy," said the Chimp, "but remember no shooting till you are sure of getting at least three of the enemy in any attack. Immediately after that you must fly to the top of a nearby building from where I can spirit you away without anyone being the wiser."

"I think tomorrow's strategy is clear to all of us and it should work fine," said Robert. "If everything goes well, will you take us to the animals in the Masai Mara?"

"Most certainly I will," answered the Chimp. "I am sure everything will go well. We will make at least a dozen attacks. In between we will take a short break and you can you can fly over the Masai Mara area and see the wild life."

That evening Henry and Robert used their magical computers to pinpoint a large number of clusters of enemy homes all over Africa. The next day they made fifteen attacks on these clusters, on the military bases and at market places. In between they flew over the Masai Mara area watching the animals. It was a breathtaking sight, watching the wildebeest, zebras, buffaloes, antelope, lions, leopards, birds and other exotic wildlife. The sheer number of animals was amazing. The children were very happy and kept repeating that it was a fabulous experience. The Chimp told them that they had knocked out over forty of the enemy. He also showed then a short scene of the Demon Jaguar conferring with his henchmen.

They heard the Demon Jaguar say, "Now I am certain that the infernal meddler is planning to invade Africa with the help of his supporters. He knows that we are too strong in America. We must try to find out who his supporters are. His game will be up the minute we find out who they are. We will crush them. Then the world will be in our hands. Numero Tres you move over from America to Africa. Your main role will be to find out the Chimps supporter's identities and I will deal with them personally. I will suck out their minds, and they will become vegetables. Numero Dos you concentrate on replacing the men you have lost, and also increasing the number of your followers. With Numero Tres helping you it should not be too difficult. I shall arrange to send your more power and weapons. Numero Uno you try to meet our target date for takeover of America. Once it is in our hands, the rest of the task will be easier."

"Yes Boss," replied Numero Uno. "I will not let you down."

The Chimp said, "We have succeeded in fooling them. Let us take a break tomorrow and meet on Tuesday evening to make plans for the future."

❖❖❖

Chapter 16

THE BATTLE PLAN

On Tuesday evening the five friends and the Chimp met in the tree house. The latter set the ball rolling by saying, "We have done well so far. Now is the right time to make the plan to knock the Big Belly out of America for a big home run." Henry responded, "We must continue with our attacks on Africa, otherwise the enemy will suspect that our real target is USA."

"You are right." said the Chimp. "We must keep up with the deception, and not make any mistake which will attract their attention to our activities in America."

"In our future raids in Africa we must be extra careful, so that the Sly Mesmer doesn't detect us and find out our identities," said Henry. "Also targets will bc scarce now, so it does not make sense for all of us to go on each raid."

"I agree. From now on I will take only one of you on each raid," said the Chimp. "I will convert myself into a flying carpet with one of you lying on my back. I will be invisible to people on the ground and no one can see you through me, or shoot you through me. You can see through the carpet but not shoot through it. When you spot a target just tap the carpet, and I will slow down, so that you can take aim and shoot. Then I will take you away from that spot before the Sly Mesmer can reach there."

"Don't you think that we need some practice shooting from a flying carpet," asked Robert.

"Oh, I don't think so," replied the Chimp. "At first you may miss a few shots, but then you will get a hang of it. Just be careful not to fall off from my back, when I whisk you out of the area after a successful shot. We shall try to shoot at least a dozen people on each raid. That will keep the Sly Mesmer on his toes, and give a lot of pain to the Wicked Don."

The Chimp continued, "I want to play a trick on these two, and their men to mislead and demoralise them. Henry, I will send you to visit them in the form of a ghostly spirit. You should try to convince them, that they are being attacked by an alliance of spirits of this world, and dead people from other worlds. Tell them that they are doomed and so must flee from this world at the earliest."

"Won't it be dangerous for Henry?" asked Marie, "They could kill him or discover his real identity."

"No, he will be perfectly safe," said the Chimp. "I will only send the image of the spirit while Henry will be right here with us. The spirit image will say what Henry says, and also mimic his every movement and even the facial expressions. We will do that on an evening ten days from today. Both of them will be in Zimbabwe, which is their main base of operations. They have planned a meeting with their top men in a cave which serves as their headquarters. The spirit will have a flaming red body while its eyes will be coal black. Its voice will be a deep, bass, computer generated voice which will induce fear in the men. Henry you must plan what you are going to say and also decide on suitable facial gestures to scare the daylights out of their men. The rest of you must help him practice, as if he is preparing for a challenging role in a school drama. I think a good performance will help our cause."

"I think Henry can handle it well" said Marie. "Last term he played the lead role in our school play, and the Bentonville newspaper gave him an excellent review."

"I know. That is why I decided on this," said the Chimp. "You all help him write out some scary dialog, and we can now plan what to do next in America."

"We do not want a long drawn out campaign here in America," said Henry. "I suggest that we attack the enemy when they meet at desolate Park. According to you, if we shoot a sufficiently large number of his men in a short time, the Wicked Don will be knocked out by the pain and his unconscious body will fly away to the Demon Jaguar. I suppose the same must be true for the Big Belly. We can shoot a very large number of his men when they gather at Ghostly Hollow. That should be enough to drive him out of USA."

"Basically you are right, but it is not as simple as that," the Chimp countered. "There are many ifs and buts involved. Also we should try for a complete victory with all of its benefits."

"Could you explain what you mean," enquired Henry.

"If the battle starts off in your favor, the top leaders under the Big Belly may order the men to disperse. They will run away in all directions, and you won't be able to shoot enough of them to ensure that the Big Belly is knocked out of America. Another complication may arise due to the powerful evil spirit that resides there. It will try to help the enemy, but then there is a good spirit in the lake, which will certainly help you. It will come to your help in case you are losing the battle, or if the evil spirit starts helping the enemy. While you are battling it out with the enemy, I will take Marie on a flying carpet ride to shoot and destroy the main enemy transmitters. This will destroy their links with all other parts of the world, and also stop the broadcasting of their evil mind control waves. Demon Jaguar should not find out anything otherwise he will intervene during the battle."

"To prevent those men from running away, we should first shoot their top leaders, who have the authority to order them to run away," said Henry. "You should tell us how to identify them."

"You also talked about a complete victory and all its benefits," said Marie. "What do you mean by that?"

"Four of the top five leaders will be on the stage, so you can easily shoot them. The topmost one, as you know, is General Grant's wife. She won't be there, because the men think that the General is their leader. The Big Belly has not been able to take control of his mind."

He paused and continued, "Regarding Marie's question, we want to free all of the men at Ghostly Hollow from the control of the Big Belly, and get hold all of their weapons. You will have to approach the General for help. His soldiers will surround Ghostly Hollow, and not let any of the enemy escape. The soldiers must also collect all of the enemy weapons, and use them later on for the mopping up operations all over the USA. After that they must eliminate each and every enemy soldier from North American and get their weapons. This is what I mean by complete victory."

"I understand that every enemy soldier in North America must be neutralised and we should collect of their weapons," Marie replied. "Then we will have so many weapons that we can think of attacking the enemy in South America."

"That is exactly what I want," replied the Chimp, "but don't count your chickens before they are hatched. Right now let us just think about the present goal, which is winning the battle of Ghostly Hollow. Victory in USA and North America will be the immediate next steps. Those are very big tasks which you five cannot carry out. The main role there will be played by General Grant and his troops, but they will need your help in identifying the enemy all over North America. This is a big task so you should start collecting the names and address of as many of the enemy as you can."

Henry raised some objections, "It won't be easy to approach the General. We can infect his computer systems, and then get to meet him like we did in case of the Mayor and the Sheriff, but why should he believe our story about the Big Belly and Demon Jaguar and their attempt to take over America. Also, they must be monitoring the General closely, and there is the risk that the Big Belly will find out the truth about us. Another complication is that, at the start of the battle, someone may send a message to the General's wife about your attacks, and she may order her men to disperse and run away from Ghostly Hollow."

"That's why meeting the General is essential," answered the Chimp. "He will believe you if you gain his confidence. During your meeting with him tell him about me, and I will make an appearance and talk with him. That should convince him."

"There may be hidden bugs in his office, which may reveal everything to the enemy," protested Henry. "They might even monitor his thoughts later, and discover our plans."

"The General is one of the few individuals whose thoughts they cannot monitor or influence," countered the Chimp. "When you talk with him about the Demon Jaguar please make sure there is no one else inside the room. I will use my magic to protect the room against bugs. There are bugs in his room which transmit images as well as conversation. My magic will ensure that these bugs do not transmit what happens there. Instead they will transmit a normal harmless conversation about computer viruses. This magical control will last for only half an hour. We will give him a magical computer, a magical pen and a ray gun and other magical gifts that I gave you. The computer and the pen will be used to coordinate our plans. The computer will also contain details of what we expect him to do. He will use the telescope of his ray gun to weed out the enemy from among his soldiers whom he sends to Ghostly Hollow. When you are about to start the attack he must use the gun to knock out his wife. Exact timing is essential. If he knocks out his wife too early then the Big Belly may suspect, and if he is late she might get a message from Ghostly Hollow and order the men to disperse."

"That is a brilliant plan," said Marie. "Even Brave Lion could not have made a better plan."

The Chimp glowed with satisfaction, but Henry had another question, "How on earth will the General use the telescope to weed out the enemy without arousing suspicion."

"These are the details that you have to work out later with the General," replied the Chimp. "Now you must plan out what to say to the General at the first meeting."

"I think this whole matter of meeting with the General, and getting his help will require very careful planning and execution," replied Henry. "I agree with Marie that your plan is brilliant. Now it is up to us to make sure that it succeeds."

❖❖❖

Chapter 17

THE FLAMING SPIRIT

That night Henry used Jack Darwin's identity to send an email to the General's office, advertising his ability to remove the most stubborn and latest viruses from any computer system. He decided to wait a few days before sending the virus. He was aware that playing the role of the Flaming Spirit well would require practice, but meeting the General was far more difficult and crucial for success in the battle against the enemy. He thought that first the office staff would try to remove the virus by themselves, and then would get outside help failing which they would approach him. By that time the visit of the Flaming Spirit to Africa would be over and done with. He reasoned that it would not be wise for all of them to visit the General and so only he and Robert would go there as Jack Darwin and Pedro Diaz respectively.

His main concerns were that the General may not be in his office, when they visited, or he might refuse to meet them. After all a general is a high ranking officer, and his time is valuable. Why should he waste his time meeting a couple of computer engineers? He would probably not bother about them and let his staff handle the matter. So Henry rang up Robert and expressed his doubts. The latter suggested, "When they ring you, to ask for your help, tell them that you are on the west coast and will undertake the long journey to the east coast only because you are a fan of the General. You must insist that they should let you and an assistant to be photographed with the General, and he must autograph the photos."

"Good idea. It is bound to work," said Henry, "but we have to make sure that they let us have a private talk with him."

"Tell them that you are also a freelance journalist," replied Robert, "and insist that you want a short private interview with him. Also say that you won't charge the travel expenses and fee for removing the virus, but want his permission to sell the interview to any magazine you decide on."

"That is another brilliant idea from you," said Henry. "I don't want to sound pessimistic, but the General may say that he can spare only five or ten minutes for the interview."

"Oh, that should be okay," replied Robert. "Leave the rest to the Chimp. He can use his magic to get us more time, or even stretch five minutes to thirty minutes. You know he compressed several days into an hour when we went on the journey to the past."

"Why didn't I think of that? You have been of great help today, so maybe you can suggest how to raise the topic of the Demon Jaguar with the General?" Henry asked.

"Tell him directly, and no beating about the bush," replied Robert. "He is a very intelligent man. I am sure he will believe what you tell him. Don't forget we have the Chimp as a trump card. If we cannot convince the General, he will surely do it."

"Thanks," said Henry. "Today you have removed a big load from my head. I was really worried about how to tackle the General. Now I can think clearly about writing the script for the Flaming Spirit, and also concentrate on acting its part." In a few minutes Henry had completed the script and was soon fast asleep.

The next evening the friends met in the tree house. Henry told them about Robert's suggestions for arranging the meeting with the General. They all agreed that his ideas were very sound. Marie said, "I am relieved that I do not have to be present at the meeting with the General, So much depends on the result of the meeting, that it makes me nervous to even think about it."

Then Henry took out the sheet of paper with the script, and read it out and they all liked it. He said that he would put it on the diary, and they could suggest changes. At this stage, the Chimp surprised the friends by making an unexpected appearance. He said, "I know everything that you have decided, and agree that Robert's suggestions are brilliant and are sure to work. The script is also really good, but how will you react when they interrupt the spirit?"

"I will react by laughing loudly," said Henry. "That will give me a few seconds to think up a suitable reply. My laugh will have the right degree of scorn and menace. It will annoy and unnerve them." After this he emitted a loud laugh, "Ha! Ha! Ha!"

"That's just right," said the Chimp. "You are doing fine. When Henry and Robert interview the General, I will make my appearance at the right moment, but I will also take Marie, John and Diego with me. That will make it easier to convince the General. Now I will leave, and meet you again here on Saturday morning at 10 am. Then we will send the Flaming Spirit to Zimbabwe. You have plenty of time to rehearse your act. Tomorrow you should infect the General's computer systems." After this the Chimp vanished.

The next few days Henry played the role of the spirit, under the watchful eyes of his friends, who helped him improve his act by suggesting changes in his hand gestures and facial expressions. Marie added some dialog in French to impress the enemy men from former French colonies. During rehearsal they also interrupted Henry as the enemy would. After some practice he could handle the interruptions smoothly. Henry also hacked into the General's office computer systems and injected the incurable viruses. On Saturday morning they assembled in the tree house and the Chimp arrived punctually at 10 am.

"The Wicked Don and the Sly Mesmer are meeting the leaders from most of the African countries," said the Chimp. "They are planning how to deal with our attacks, which have affected the morale of their followers. Now I will show you what is going on at their meeting in Zimbabwe." Immediately the friends saw a scene inside a vast cave. There was an oblong table with two men, the Wicked Don and the Sly Mesmer seated on one short side with their backs towards the friends, and a large number of men on the other three sides. Some were wearing traditional Arab robes, others were dressed as Masai warriors, Zulus, Tuaregs etcetera and some were in military uniforms. It looked like a costume party, but the friend's knew that these were the men who would be ruling in their countries once they were captured by the enemy. The Wicked Don was addressing the men who were listening with rapt attention.

The Chimp said to Henry, "When I send the spirit into the cave, you will feel as if you are there and you will see through its eyes and hear through its ears. They may shoot at you with their weapons, but that won't hurt you, so don't show any fear. The act will be yours for most of the time, but when the situation arises, I may take control of the spirit and create some special effects. The rest of us will sit here and enjoy your performance." Then he gestured with his hand and the Flaming Spirit appeared in the cave and the Chimp said to Henry, "Start your act."

The Flaming Spirit was flaming red and scary and so large that its head almost touched the cave roof. It startled many of the men who rose from their chairs in fright, and were about to run away. The Wicked Don and the Sly Mesmer turned around and were surprised by what they saw but recovered quickly. The former shouted, "There is nothing to fear while we are here. This is a trick being played by the infernal meddling enemy."

The spirit laughed loudly, "Ha! Ha! Ha!" The sound echoed for some time, frightening the men even more. The spirit continued, "Run away while you can, otherwise you will be hunted down like vermin. This is my first and last warning to you. So far we have spared the lives of your men, but from now on anyone who sides with these two evil beings will be killed without mercy. As for you two, go and tell your evil master that I, the ruling spirit of this world, have summoned all of my subjects and many of my allies from other worlds. You stand no earthly chance against our combined forces. Flee while you can, otherwise you and your master will be marooned as prisoners on this world for eternity."

Then he repeated some of it in French. Hearing his words some of the men tried to flee but the Sly Mesmer waved his hand, and the men halted in their tracks. The Wicked Don shouted at the spirit, "You had better flee from this cave before my men shoot you down." Then he addressed his men, "It is only a balloon sent by our enemy. Shoot at it and watch it shrivel in size."

Many of the men picked up their ray guns or took out ray pistols or normal hand guns from their holsters, and started shooting at the spirit. Henry controlled himself, and remained immobile so that the spirit also remained immobile. Then the spirit laughed again and said, "Shoot as much as you like. It will have no effect on me." The men stopped shooting and the

Wicked Don said, "You had better escape before I suck the life out of you." Then he made a sucking motion with his mouth. The spirit remained unmoved, laughed loudly and said with mock seriousness, "You are planning to conquer Africa, but are so stupid that you do not even know that a spirit has no life, so how can you suck it out. I warn you that my followers will keep inflicting very painful pinpricks on your body every day."

"Your pinpricks do not bother me," retorted the Wicked Don. "My skin is very thick."

"I know that pigs have thick skins," the Flaming Spirit countered. "Even so the pinpricks have caused you much pain in the past. I have seen you rolling on the ground many times and writhing in pain. The scenes were so funny that every time I laughed very loudly. If I had been a human being then surely my stomach would have burst with laughter."

The Sly Mesmer said, "You claim to be the ruler of all spirits, yet many of them are on our side. See if you can fight them." He gestured and three small, misty, evil spirits appeared and flew swiftly towards the Flaming Spirit and entered its chest and emerged from its back. This caused Henry to flinch in surprise and the Flaming Spirit also flinched. The Sly Mesmer laughed loudly and said, "Even the great ruling spirit of this world is afraid of three of our tiniest spirits. If our larger spirits attack, you will probably die of fright."

The Flaming Spirit replied, "They passed harmlessly through me and I felt nothing." Then it gestured with its right arm and a swarm of luminous cockroaches flew towards the enemy. Instinctively the Wicked Don and the Sly Mesmer ducked to the ground, while some of their men tried to swat the cockroaches, which were the special effects created by the Chimp. For many of the men, the last few minutes had been rather frightening, and the appearance of the cockroaches was the last straw, which sent them running madly out of the cave. The Flaming Spirit laughed again. This time more loudly and heartily than before and said, "You startled me a bit by suddenly hurling three evil spirits at me, but a handful of my ghostly cockroaches scared the daylights out of you and your men. How will you react if a horde of ghostly elephants, lions, and rhinos attacks?"

On hearing this, the remaining men also dashed out of the cave leaving the Wicked Don and The Sly Mesmer alone with the Flaming Spirit, which continued, "Let this be a lesson to you. Your men, whom you have chosen to be the future rulers in their countries, have run away like a pack of jackals. They may be miles away by now. I will leave now because you will be busy chasing them to try and bring them back." Then the Flaming Spirit vanished, and the scene slowly faded away. Back in the tree house the Chimp said, "Now that was the funniest scene that I have seen. Henry surely deserves an Oscar for his acting." After this they all roared with laughter. Then Henry said to the Chimp, "You also deserve credit for sending the ghostly cockroaches and threatening to send elephants, lions and rhinos after them."

Meanwhile their loud laughter had been heard in the main house. Mrs. Taylor commented, "Something very funny must have happened." Her daughter Joan said, "Oh, it must be some silly joke which one of them told. I never see anything funny in any of their jokes."

Henry appeared to be puzzled. He said, "That part about them being marooned on this world for eternity was not a part of my script, so why did I say it?"

"It was something that I added," said the Chimp. "When I travel from one world to another I do not consume any energy. But the Demon Jaguar needs the mental power he collects from the people in order to travel from one world to another. Without him his assistants cannot go from one world to another by themselves. He has to carry them. I always keep hoping that one day his power dips down so low that he and his assistants are all marooned on a planet. We have had countless encounters, but it has never happened so far. He is too clever. Whenever he is losing and his power goes down he escapes to some other world taking his assistants with him. It is probably destined that he and I will oppose each other for all times to come."

"You never told us about this before," said Marie. "I have a question. Can he or his gang members actually suck out the life from a person?"

"He and his men can suck out life from a person but it makes them very weak and dizzy, and they need a long time to regain strength," replied the Chimp. "That is they do it only in an emergency."

"How is it that you know so much about him," continued Marie, "but he and his men know so little about you?"

"I must thank the ruler of nature for giving me that advantage," replied the Chimp. "I have been given some more advantages. Demon Jaguar and his men cannot locate me, but can only vaguely sense my presence. I can locate them and also show you what they are doing. After one of our fights is over, he does not remember the finer details of tactics that I used against him, but I remember his tactics. It seems that when he travels from one world to another he and his men forget much."

❖❖❖

Chapter 18

INTERVIEWING THE GENERAL

Henry had hoped that the General's office would contact him soon. Each night he would go to bed disappointed and toss and turn in his bed for a long time before falling asleep. His friends advised him to be patient. Marie said, "No one else can get rid of the virus from their computers. They are bound to call you in a few days." Meanwhile the daily attacks on the enemy in Africa were continued. Each day the Chimp would transform himself into an invisible flying carpet, and one of the friends would lie on it and shoot as many of the enemy as possible. Marie enjoyed it the most. She knocked out more enemies than anyone else because she never missed a target. She beamed with joy when the Chimp said that she was as good as Anne Oakley.

After many agonising days Henry got the much awaited call from the General's office. The voice on the line enquired, "Are you Jack Darwin?" Henry replied, "No, I am his nephew. Please hold a minute while I give him the phone." Then he transformed himself into Jack Darwin and spoke in the voice of an adult. By the time the call was over, Henry felt exhilarated. He immediately contacted his friends, and told them that the General's office had agreed to let him and an associate interview the General if they could remove the virus. The next day the Chimp transported the friends to a place near the General's office so that Henry and Robert could reach there in time for the visit. As soon as they entered the building and stated their business, they were led to the computers. In a short while they removed the virus, and were taken to the General's room and introduced to him.

He thanked them warmly and said, "Gentlemen, you have done what a lot of experts failed to do. I am most grateful to you. Normally I don't like being interviewed, but in your case it will give me great pleasure. Now go ahead and ask me whatever you want. Henry looked meaningfully at the secretary and aide who were present in the room. The General said, "Oh, don't worry about them. They are present at all of my top secret meetings."

Henry replied, "It is not a question of secrecy. It's just that it upsets our style of interviewing when an audience is present."

The General shrugged his shoulders and remarked, "Let's do it your way." Then he motioned to the secretary and the aide to leave the room, and told them not to let anyone enter while the interview was in progress. As soon as these two had exited, Henry came straight to the point, "My friend Pedro and I want to talk with you about what happened in South America and what is going on here."

The General replied, "Sorry, I do not want to discuss that because most of it is top secret. You may ask me anything else." Then he pointed with his finger to the four walls of the room and then towards his ears. Henry understood the meaning of his gesture and said, "Let me assure you that, before entering, we have taken care to neutralise all possible audio visual bugging devices that may have been planted in your office. Also we do not want to ask you anything. In fact we want to give you an authentic version of what actually happened in South America and how it happened."

The General was surprised and said, "You are computer wizards, but how could you possibly neutralise hidden bugging devices before entering my room? It is just not possible. What makes you so sure that you know what really happened in South America? Even the government, with all its resources, is still trying to figure out what happened there. You can't possibly know more than us."

"Yes, we are sure we know a lot more than you," asserted Henry. "We know that a powerful alien being and his helpers have conquered South America, and are now trying to conquer North America. We also have a plan to foil them."

The General laughed, "You are right about the alien beings, but how can you hope to beat them, when even we in the army are clueless about it? No harm in listening to your plan. At the worst I may get a laugh out of it." This annoyed Henry, who retorted angrily, "We removed your computer viruses when all the other experts had failed. Doesn't that mean anything at all?"

The General apologised, "Sorry, I meant no offence. It's just that I have been under a lot of stress lately as we really do not know how to tackle these alien beings. Their weapons and technology are way ahead of ours. Go ahead, tell me your plan. I am all ears."

This mollified Henry and he continued, "It is a long story so I shall give you only the essential parts. A few months ago a good alien whom we call the Chimp, came to the earth and told us and three more of our friends all about these alien beings and their intention to enslave our planet for their evil purpose. This would mean the end of civilisation as it exists. He encouraged us to fight against the invaders under his guidance."

Then Henry proceeded to tell him in brief about Demon Jaguar and his followers, and their powers, and how they had captured South America. After this, Henry told him about their own adventures starting from the journey to the past and ending with their raids in Africa, and their plan to defeat the enemy at

Ghostly Hollow. The General listened with rapt attention, asking a few questions in between. Robert made a contribution whenever he felt that Henry had missed something vital. It was only towards the end that Henry realised with a shock, that they had been in the room for more than an hour as compared to the half an hour period of safety guaranteed by the Chimp.

The General said, "Your story is very interesting but strange. I would like to believe it but I am not fully convinced." At this stage the Chimp made his appearance in the same manner as he had appeared for the first time in Henry's room, and spoke to the startled General, "My appearance will make you believe the starting part of their story. Now I will call their three friends." Diego, Marie and John appeared in the same manner in the forms of Stan Gonzalez, Jane Kennedy and Wayne Butler, and the Chimp continued, "General, this completes the five friends who will battle the enemy at Ghostly Hollow. They will transform into children right in front of you, and this will make you believe another part of the story."

One by one they transformed themselves into their true selves, and the Chimp said, "The enemy is not monitoring the thoughts of children. These are five of the bravest and most talented children and the best I could have chosen. You are one of the few men whose thoughts cannot be monitored by the enemy hence their secret is safe with you, however, without your support, we cannot win the war here in the USA. Please help them." The General replied, "Now I am ready to believe everything, but I am not sure that your plan will succeed. I am willing to give all help and support and even lay down my life if required."

"That is the last thing we would want," said the Chimp. "Victory in the USA is only the beginning. After this we must eliminate the enemy from North America and finally from the world. Without you and your soldiers, that will be impossible. So I don't want you to sacrifice your life. I will give you the same magical gifts and the super powers that I have given to these children, and train you in their use."

Then he raised his hand and one by one the magical gifts kept appearing, and he kept giving them to the General. Finally he gave him a ray gun, a ray pistol and a pair of special sun glasses and said, "The gun sight and the sun glasses will help you identify the enemy. Now for the biggest surprise of all, your wife's mind has been taken over by the enemy. They could not take control of your mind, so they did the next best thing. Once they capture power in the USA they will drug you and declare you as the ruler. In reality it will be your wife who will rule but the people will think that you are the ruler."

On hearing this, the General expressed no surprise. He said, "I believe you. She has been behaving strangely for quite some time, trying to spy on me, taking an undue interest in my work, and going through my papers secretly. She even said to me a couple of times, that it would be wonderful if we could jointly rule over the country. I would be the Emperor and she would be the Empress. At that time I felt that she was in need of psychiatric treatment, but now I understand everything. What should I do about her?"

"Just act normally," said the Chimp. "We don't want the enemy to know that you suspect anything fishy." He was about to say something more but Henry interrupted him and said, "Our safe period was over long ago."

"Don't worry," said the Chimp. "I have adjusted the time and we have only spent ten minutes in terms of real time." Then he turned towards the General and said "You will use the ray pistol to knockout your wife when these boys start the attack on Ghostly Hollow. Perfect timing is essential. We also want that you should take about a hundred men to seal of the escape route from Ghostly Hollow. Take care to ensure that none of your men are possessed by the enemy. The mission should be secret so that none of these men know beforehand where they are going and what they have to do. As soon as these boys defeat the enemy and knock the Big Belly out of the USA, you must move in with half of your men to collect the weapons and knockout the remaining enemy. Your remaining men will be on guard to stop the enemy from fleeing. In the coming few days you and these boys must keep in contact to coordinate the attack."

"What about the rest of enemy in the USA and the rest of North America?" asked the General?

"You and yours soldiers will have to eliminate them. These children will help you", replied the Chimp. "That task must be completed within a month of the Big Belly being knocked out of here because it will take him about that much time to recover his powers and regain control of his men in North America."

"Can't the Demon Jaguar or the other gang members gain control of the men?" asked the General.

"No, they cannot unless the Big Belly transfers them to their control," replied the Chimp, "When we attack at Ghostly Hollow we will also destroy their entire communication network in North America and their broadcasters which broadcast the controlling waves. This will make your task easier. These children will give you the names and addresses of the enemy men and women all over North America," said the Chimp.

"I will need to discuss this with the POTUS and take his approval. He will also have to get in touch with the Prime Ministers and Presidents of all the countries in North America to let me and my troops enter their countries to deal with the enemy", said the General. "How do we do all of this secretly without alerting the enemy".

"Yes, that is a good question", replied the Chimp. "Do you have any suggestion?"

"After three days, I'm supposed to meet the POTUS for a routine meeting," said the General, "I can discuss everything then but your help will be needed to keep it secret from the enemy."

"That can be arranged," said the Chimp. "At that meeting, you can discuss whatever you like with the POTUS. All others present their will not hear what you say. Instead they will hear something harmless. Now, if these are no more questions or suggestions from any of you, we can end the meeting".

"Not right now", said the General, "but how do I get in touch with you if I want to ask you something."

"Just close your eyes and repeat my name twice and I will appear before you", replied the Chimp.

"Alright," said the General, "now let me summarise our battle plan. Correct me where I am wrong. You and these children will collect the names, addresses, phone numbers and mobile numbers of enemy's men and the locations of their arms storage. You will also continue with the attacks on Africa to divert attention from USA which is our real target. You will teach me the use of these weapons and devices and provide suitable deception at the meeting with the POTUS. I will collect a hundred reliable soldiers for the operation on D-day when these children attack the enemy at Ghostly Hollow. When I get the signal, I must knockout my wife with this ray pistol. Once the enemy is routed my men must collect all the enemy's men and their weapons. After that we have about a month's time to wipe out the remaining enemy soldiers from USA and the rest of North America and seize all of their weapons."

"That is our plan in a nutshell," said the Chimp, and everyone nodded in agreement except Marie who said, "When we attack Africa let us also fly a few sorties over Europe shooting up some of the enemy. That will really confuse the Demon Jaguar and his gang."

"She's saying this because she wants to see the sights in Europe," said Robert.

"That is a great idea Marie," said the Chimp. "I will take you on these sorties to Europe and let you see the changing of guard at the Buckingham Palace, and show you the Eifel Tower, the Leaning Tower of Pisa and anything else which you want to see."

"I want to see all of these and Mount Blanc also," replied Marie.

"There is one more detail," said the General. "I feel that these children alone will find it very difficult to defeat the enemy at Ghostly Hollow. If you give me a few more ray guns then I will arm some of my men who will take part in the battle."

"We can spare three guns," replied the Chimp, "Each of these kids must carry a spare gun with them. You can only give these guns to the soldiers after the battle starts. I will also give you three wrist watches which they must wear in order to have immunity, otherwise the very first enemy shot will kill them. Also they won't get time to learn to fly and will have to shoot from the ground."

"I feel relieved," said Henry. "We need all the help we can get."

❖❖❖

Chapter 19

STARTING THE BATTLE

The next few days were filled with feverish activity, with everyone going about their assigned tasks in earnest. The Chimp flew Marie on a large number of sorties over Africa and Europe where she shot many enemies. This had the desired effect. It convinced the enemy that the war would be fought there, and attention was diverted away from America. The Chimp rewarded her by showing her the sights which he had promised her. She saw a breathtaking view of Mont Blanc. The Leaning tower of Pisa intrigued her. The Eifel tower was marvelous and the changing of the guard at Buckingham palace was impressive. Each was magnificent in its own way. What more could she ask for!

Henry and the others collected the names, addresses, phone numbers and email ids of the enemy's people in all of North America and transmitted this information to the General's computer. They also flew high above Ghostly Hollow to study its topography and kept in regular touch with the General and the Chimp to ensure that everything was proceeding according to their plan. The Chimp taught the General all that he had taught the children, including how to fly. He also provided him with protection against the enemy ray guns, and gave him another identity in the body of a hero from another world known as Black Bear.

He said, “After we win the battle of Ghostly Hollow on D-day, the enemy may find out that you are directing the battle for the USA and North America. He may try to kill you by sending teams from South America, Africa or Europe to assassinate you. If they succeed, we will lose the war for North America. After Ghostly Hollow is won you must take the identity of Black. Bear. As long as the wars for USA and North America last you should remain in this body most of the time. So that the enemy cannot locate your position.”

“Then how do you expect me to command my soldiers when they can’t recognise me?” The General enquired.

“You will remain in hiding in a secret cave with a few aides to help you. All communications between you and your troops will be through a secure wifi network.” said the Chimp. “I have located such a cave, and have stocked it with everything that you will need.”

“What if the Demon Jaguar sends a large invasion force from South America?” asked the General.

“You should place the army, the navy and the air force on alert to guard against that possibility,” replied the Chimp, “but the chances of a full scale invasion are small. Firstly that is not his style. More importantly he knows that if he sends an invasion force the ships will all be sunk and the planes will all be shot down, and the entire invading party will be killed, since his conventional weaponry is no match for yours. Like I said earlier, he may try to sneak in small groups of men by motor boats or by light aircraft.”

“Oh, I see,” responded the General. The Chimp continued, “The Wicked Don or the Sly Mesmer may send theirs assassins from Africa or Europe or anywhere else by normal airline flights. These men will try to assassinate you, the POTUS or leaders of other North American countries. In the meantime the Big Belly may recover and hand over control of his soldiers to the Inquisitor or to some other gang member. Then these people will create a lot of problems for us and we may lose the war. Both you and the POTUS are essential for our victory."

"You have explained everything so well that I understand the whole situation," replied the General. "I will explain everything to the POTUS. I assure you that he has a very sharp mind, and will do whatever is necessary to defeat the enemy." The Chimp replied, "That is excellent. I will provide protection to the POTUS after your meeting with him. I will give him a secure place for the duration of the war in North American. He can work from there and come out only for short periods when it is essential. If you or the POTUS need my help or anymore information be sure to ask me."

The General's meeting with the POTUS was held under the cover of secrecy created by the Chimp. He told the latter about everything including what was planned on D-day. The latter listened with keen interest and interrupted the General from time to time to ask relevant questions. At the end of it all he closed his eyes and remained silent for a while as if in a trance. The General was worried that the POTUS had not believed what he was told and it had upset him.

After a couple of minutes, the President opened his eyes and said, "If anyone else had told me this, I would have said that it is the greatest load of rubbish that I have heard in a long time. Coming from you, I believe every word you said. I just analysed the facts in my mind and everything makes sense." The General said, "For a minute you had me worried. I thought that you didn't believe what I said."

"My fuzzy minded advisers had misguided me all this while," continued the POTUS. "Now the picture is clear to me. I have full faith in you, the Chimp and those five children. I will send my advisers on leave and rely totally on you and the Chimp for advice. You all have my permission to defeat the enemy in whatever way you can. I will issue whatever orders you need for this purpose. I will also tell my staff to follow whatever orders you give to them directly. I am concerned about those five brave children. Just make sure that they come out of the war safe and sound."

The General advised the POTUS to put the army, navy and the air force on alert for a possible invasion by the Demon Jaguar's forces from South America, and to get in touch with the heads of governments of other North American countries around D-day the 4th of July.

After returning to his office, he also asked for four hundred volunteers from his troops and divided them into four groups making sure that one of these groups did not have any of the enemy's men. He intended to use this group at Ghostly Hollow. The other three were to be sent on decoy operations in other parts of the USA.

As D-day approached, Henry and the boys became increasingly tense. The former was unable to sleep well at night. He said, "I haven't been able to sleep well for so many nights that I am worried that I might fall asleep during the battle on D-day." John said, "Sometimes I also feel the pressure and don't get good sleep at night." Marie, on the other hand, did not have any such problem. She said, "If you follow my advice, you will be fine. Always remember you have immunity. At worst you will be shot a few times during the battle, and it will hurt like hell, but you won't die."

"You are mistaken," retorted Henry. "We are not afraid of the pain. It is just that so much is at stake that we don't want to make some silly mistake and lose the battle. That is what worries me and keeps me awake all night."

"Then it's just a question of nerves," said Marie. "When you are upset try deep breathing and meditate with your eyes closed for a few minutes. Try some yogic exercises for relaxation if you know them. Else look them up on the net. They should soothe your nerves, and you will sleep better."

"You may be right," said John. "Let's all give it a try. Maybe it will work."

Marie continued, "Remember we have the advantage of surprise. Our planning has been so thorough that we have covered every possibility. Besides, we have magical powers. Even the General and his men will help us. The President will order his staff to do whatever the General tells them. I believe that the odds favor us a hundred to one. You guys just have to hold your nerves and the battle will be ours to win."

"Thanks for the pep talk," replied Henry. "From now on we four must think positively like you."

The friends had flown over Ghostly Hollow to survey the area. It was an elliptical depression ringed by a low range of hills, being about a mile wide and one and a half miles long. At one point there was a break in the hills like a pass. A paved road sloped down into the area through this pass, and ended at a flat raised plateau like area almost circular in shape and about five hundred yards in diameter. It had large trees around its periphery from where the land sloped gently to the lower areas of the hollow. The road had been constructed and the trees planted there when it was used as a fair ground. At the lowest point of the hollow there was the lake with bushes and trees around it.

The whole area was dotted with trees and bushes here and there with vast open spaces. The area had seen better days, but the road had been repaired and the plateau spruced up in preparation for their fair. A couple of days before D-day a large number of tables, chair, booths and other stalls used in fairs had been brought there and arranged suitably. Some tents were erected. A day later decorative banners, flags and flower pots were placed there. Early morning on D-day the fourth of July, balloons of many colors were tied to stakes driven in the ground. It gave the appearance of a fair.

Later the forces of evil started arriving at Ghostly Hollow. They had travelled, a couple of days earlier, in small groups, from all over USA and had checked into hotels and motels or stayed on camping grounds in the small towns and cities nearby. These men and women were among the top persons in their own areas, and were dressed casually to avoid drawing attention. Many of them carried the ray gun or pistol kits concealed in their bags. They drove down to Ghostly Hollow in buses. Some more ray guns were brought concealed in secret compartments built inside the busses. Suitable precautions were taken to make sure that only their own people boarded these buses, which dropped them at the entrance where guards made another security check. After unloading its passengers and the concealed guns each bus sped back to bring more of the enemy.

Soon the plateau in the middle of the hollow was teeming with thousands of people. Among them there were food stalls, souvenir shops, ice-cream vans and all other paraphernalia to make it look like a fair was in progress. There was a small wooden platform in one corner with four chairs placed on it. Soon four men mounted it and sat on these chairs. These were the leaders from the four regions of USA. Their task was to explain the overall plan for the conquest of USA and North

America and to assign individual tasks to the group leaders and other important persons who had come from all over USA. They appeared to be talking with each other, but their words were being broadcast in code by short range communicators to the crowd of people. These people were walking around among the stalls but were paying careful attention to what they were hearing on their concealed ear phones. Anyone flying over the area in a plane or a helicopter would have been fooled into thinking that a country fair was in progress. Only a very keen observer would have noticed the absence of children and become suspicious.

That same morning the friends had assembled in the woods behind Henry's house near the tree where their weapons were hidden. The Chimp gave them a short pep talk, and zipped off with them to a small hill near Ghostly Hollow where he left Henry, Robert, John and Diego saying "Good luck and good hunting." Then he zipped away taking Marie on her mission to destroy the enemy communication and broadcasting network.

The General had also prepared well for D-day. He had advised the POTUS to put the army, navy and the air force on alert after D-day for a possible invasion from South America and for infiltration parties which might come from there or Europe and Africa. On Friday night he had come to a small town near Ghostly Hollow along with his wife. He had told her that he was tired, and needed a quiet vacation. His chosen group of hundred men had assembled in a nearby military base along with a fleet of helicopters. On the fourth of July, that is D-day, he and his wife were sipping coffee while relaxing in front of the TV. He was on the alert for the signals from Henry.

Meanwhile Henry and his group were on the hill behind a bush observing the enemy through a powerful pairs of binoculars. They saw the platform on which the four leaders sat.

These would be their first targets. Henry said, "John you fly to the north side of the crowd and Diego you fly to the west. Robert and I will fly to the east and the south and knock out the four leaders. Then we will all start shooting at the rest of the crowd. We must maintain a steady rate of firing so that we keep the Big Belly off balance." He sent the alert signal to the General and Marie and flew off to shoot the leaders. Within a few seconds all four were knocked out, and Henry sent the action signal for the General and Marie.

The Chimp and Marie had been hovering near one of the main communication transmitters. On getting the action signal, Marie shot at it and neutralised it. Then they zipped to the other location and neutralised five more transmitters. "That takes care of communication with South America", said the Chimp. "Won't they suspect that something fishy is going on," asked Marie. "No," replied the Chimp. "Communications with South America are interrupted during periods of excessive solar radiations, so it's nothing unusual for them. Now let us move quickly to destroy more of their transmitters, to sabotage their communications further and also to stop broadcasting of their mind controlling rays."

On receiving the second signal, the General sent a signal to the POTUS to put the army, navy and the air force on the alert. He then shot his wife with the ray pistol and knocked her out. An army doctor and nurse took her under their care. The General summoned his men who arrived in helicopters. He explained their task and they boarded the helicopters and headed towards Desolate Hallow. All the helicopters landed behind a hill close to the entrance. Then he climbed the hill, and used the ray gun to knock out the half a dozen enemy soldiers who were standing guard at the entrance with ray guns and ray pistols. He put some of his own men to guard the entrance using the ray guns and pistols of the fallen enemy. He took a few men with him to help Henry and his friends. The rest of his men had surrounded Ghostly Hollow to cut off the escape routes of the enemy. These were armed with machine guns and had orders to shoot any enemy who attacked them.

He and the men with him moved forward along the path leading into the hollow and hid behind a boulder from where they could see the action. He then explained the use of the ray guns and the magical wrist watch to his men. He had planned to shoot at the enemy from the ground, since these men had not mastered the art of flying.

The battle was going in favor of Henry and his friends. They were flying in the air like eagles and shooting the bewildered enemy who kept falling like nine pins. Many of the enemy took out their ray gun kits from their bags, and hastily assembled them, and started firing at random, as they did not know where the shots were coming from.

Henry and his friends were elated to think that the battle would be won quite soon. They thought that Marie had been right in saying that the odds favored them heavily. They had begun well and it all seemed too easy. This created some doubts in Henry's mind, but they did not linger as his mind was preoccupied by the task on hand. They had to shoot as many of the enemy as possible, and be alert to ensure that they did not run away from the plateau. That is why the four of them were on four sides of the crowd trying to keep them confined by shooting at the people on the outer fringes.

❖❖❖

Chapter 20

THE FORTUNES OF WAR

The evil spirit of the hollow became aware of the action. It sensed that the forces of evil were being shot at by the flying eagles, and they did not know who was shooting at them. It suddenly became active. It went to the platform and picked up a mouthpiece from one of the fallen leaders, and spoke repeatedly, "Look up and see the enemy. They are flying in the guise of eagles and shooting at you."

The entire crowd was alerted. Now the ray guns were aimed at the four eagles and shooting began in earnest. The friends felt the painful strikes of the rays and almost dropped their ray guns. They started diving, twisting and turning. That helped a bit but they were still getting shot. The pain was intense. Worse still they could not shoot back effectively at the enemy. In an urgent voice Henry said to the others, "Find cover behind trees and fly away as far as you can. I will cover your retreat."

Robert, John and Diego quickly flew behind some trees, while Henry kept shooting at the enemy. Many in the crowd kept shooting at the trees behind which the three had fled, but most of the firing was directed at Henry. The pain was almost unbearable and he felt that he would faint. After his friends had taken refuge behind the trees, he too dived swiftly behind a tree. The foliage hid him from view, but he was still taking a few lucky hits, since the men kept shooting and the tree branches and leaves could not stop the rays. In desperation he sent a distress signal to the Chimp. In front of him, the ground sloped down to a small lake with some bushes growing around it. He was sure that the enemy would follow him and try to finish him off. He wanted to reach the lake and take cover behind the bushes. Then he could shoot the enemy soldiers who came looking for him, but he felt very weak. Then his mind became almost blank, everything around him became dark.

When Henry and his friend were being shot by the crowd, the General had been explaining the use of the ray guns and the wrist watches to his three men. They were dismayed to see the boys being shot at by the vast evil army. Then they saw them take painful hits and retreat behind the trees in a bid to fly out of range. By this time he and his men were ready for action. He immediately ordered them to start shooting at the enemy. After this the Chimp had received the distress signal from Henry. He said to Marie, "We must go to the help the boys otherwise all will be lost. Hold on tight and we will be off to Ghostly Hollow." They were there in the blink of an eyelid. Flying overhead on the carpet Marie was in an excellent position to shoot the enemy and she did so with gusto. Both she and the General and his men kept the score board moving enough to keep the Big Belly writhing in pain and unable to do anything.

John, Robert and Diego had flown away and come to the ground and hid behind some bushes. Some of the enemy from the crowd had followed behind each of them. By now the three had recovered from the pain, and started shooting at these men, many of whom were knocked out. Some of the others started running back while others lay on the ground and started shooting at the bushes where the three were hiding. The three were hit by a few lucky shot and felt severe pain but each time one of their shots hit an enemy, he was knocked out. However, they were able to knock out only a few of the enemy who were all lying down.

Both sides were pinned down where they were. John and the others had heard the emergency message which Henry had sent to the Chimp, and were sure that he must have arrived at the scene of the battle with Marie. They also felt that by now the General and his men must also be shooting at the enemy. John called Henry but got no reply, and was worried about his fate. He then spoke with Robert and Diego and found out that, like him, they too were pinned down behind some bushes by the enemy.

Meanwhile Henry had almost blacked out and was flying in the direction of the bushes near the lake. Suddenly he heard a voice in his mind, "I am the good spirit of this area. You must hide inside the lake. Unscrew the barrel of your gun and use it to breathe through your mouth while you remain underwater. The enemy soldiers will search for you among the bushes and will soon go away. I will tell you when to come out." These words revived him. Using his last reserves of strength, he flew into a clump of bushes and quickly unscrewed the gun barrel and lay down under water using the barrel to breathe. Only the tip protruded out of the water, and it was hidden from view by some plants on the lake edge. The good spirit converted itself into a dense fog to cover the lake. By this time the enemy soldiers had reached the bushes and started searching. They did not suspect that he was hiding in the lake. After a short while they gave up the search and headed back.

The cool water had lessened Henry's pain, his mind cleared a bit, and he lamented, "We have lost the battle and now the earth is doomed. It was extremely stupid of me to overlook this possibility."

Then he heard the voice of the good spirit in his mind, "My brave friend, do not despair. When you and your friends retreated, the General and his men and the girl took up the battle. The girl is shooting at the enemy safely from the flying carpet and the General and his men are shooting from all four sides of the plateau. Your three friends are hiding behind some bushes, and shooting at the enemy who came to kill them. You may now come out as the enemy has gone. The magical waters of the lake have given you fresh energy to resume the battle." Henry mumbled, "Thanks! You saved my life and have given me renewed hope?" The spirit said, "Get your gun ready quickly and shoot the enemy who came after you, otherwise they may shoot the General's soldier who is on this side of the plateau."

Henry reacted immediately and knocked several of the retreating enemy before they realised what was happening. Then the rest lay on the ground and started shooting towards the bushes and Henry was also pinned down. He then called John who was relieved to hear from him and told him that he and the others were similarly pinned down. Henry contacted the Chimp and asked for his help. The Chimp replied, "I will come over with Marie and hover above the enemy near you and the others. Marie will easily knock them out from above. Then all of you can move up to the plateau edge and start knocking out the main enemy crowd."

Soon Henry and the other three were free to move to the plateau edge. They hid behind some rocks or earth mounds, and would pop out after every few seconds and take a few quick shots at the enemy and hide again. By now the enemy soldiers were lying down behind their fallen comrades, or wherever they could hide. Even so sufficient were getting knocked out to keep the Big Belly paralysed with pain.

Soon the battle started swinging in favor of the enemy. The evil spirit started helping the enemy. It pointed out the hiding places of each of the boys and the General and his soldiers. Each time it would give a warning when any one of them emerged from his cover. Soon the General, his men and the boys got shot so many times that they were in severe pain and their shooting rate went down. The enemy sent groups of men crawling towards each hiding place under covering fire. They also called out to them to surrender. Henry and his friends thought that all was lost, but they went on shooting and decided to go down fighting rather than surrender.

Suddenly they saw an amazing scene. A large number of fierce dinosaurs of all sizes, had appeared out of nowhere, and were moving menacingly towards the enemy, from all around, while making frightening noises. The enemy firing was directed at the dinosaurs, but it had no effect on them. This unnerved the enemy. Their advancing enemy groups fled towards their main group, which had already started running helter-skelter like frightened ants. They had no place to run to as the dinosaurs moved slowly towards them from all directions. The evil spirit kept screaming, "It is just an illusion. Do not be afraid. Just ignore the dinosaurs and shoot at the enemy."

This reassured some of the men who tried to rally and fight back, but many others still shot at the dinosaurs which kept on moving towards them. The good spirit also got into the act. It imitated the voice of the evil spirit and shouted even louder, "They are magical dinosaurs. You can't kill them. They will eat you." This terrified many who threw away their guns and tried to retreat away from the dinosaurs. In this way they formed a small circle at the centre of the plateau.

The Chimp said to the friends, "I can hold the illusion for only a few more minutes, so make the best use of it to give the

Big Belly the knockout blow." The General, his soldiers and the friends forgot the pain, popped out of their hiding places, and started shooting at the enemy crowd in earnest. Even Marie fired with renewed determination from her perch on the flying carpet. The enemy kept falling in large numbers. Suddenly the sky brightened, the pall of gloom lifted, and Ghostly Hollow seemed to be transformed into the Sunshine Park of long ago.

The General and the five friends all sensed that the Big Belly had been knocked out and hit for a home run all the way to ULSAR. The battle was won, but they still had to knockout the remaining enemy to free them from the control of evil. So they kept on shooting at anyone who stood or moved. The General called in more of his men and told them to pick up the enemy's ray guns and knock out the remaining enemy. Then he, his soldiers and the friends sat down to take a well-earned rest.

The General sent the unconscious people to hospitals for recovery and rehabilitation. Some of these were injured, having sustained cuts, bruises and fractures on being trampled by their comrades. Fortunately none were killed. The ray guns were collected from the battlefield by his soldiers for use against the enemy.

During the next few days a large number of soldiers were trained in the use of the enemies' weapons. Some of the telescopic sights of the guns were installed at airports to check for enemy infiltrators. Within a week all of the Big Belly's people were located and neutralised and their weapons were recovered from all over the USA. The POTUS had contacted the governments of other North American countries to keep them informed about the latest developments. They all agreed to let US troops enter their countries to conduct joint operations with their soldiers to eliminate the enemy. The General, in his guise of Black Wolf, coordinated these operations from his secret cave so well that within eighteen days the entire continent of North America was free of all enemy soldiers. They had got the complete victory that the Chimp had wanted.

All this while, the Demon Jaguar could not do anything effective. He ranted and raved and cursed the Chimp for all he was worth. In desperation he sent a few groups of men by motor boats but they were neutralised by soldiers waiting for them on the shores. Some other men were sent from Africa and Europe but were caught and neutralised at the airports where they landed. The Big Belly had not recovered from the severe pain inflicted on him during the D-day battle. He could neither issue instructions to the people under his control, nor could he transfer their control to some other gang members or to the Demon Jaguar. The latter decided not to risk sending a full scale invading party to help the men in North America. He knew that the invasion would fail, because their ships would be sunk and their planes would be shot down and his men would be killed or captured.

❖❖❖

EPILOGUE

They all knew that the battle for North America had been won, but it was not a time for rejoicing. Still a lot remained to be done. South America was firmly in the hands of the Demon Jaguar. He had considerable strength in Africa and some influence in Europe and other parts of the world. It would be a tough battle to drive out Demon Jaguar and his men from the earth.

A grateful POTUS ordered the creation of special medals for extreme bravery and service to the nation and to humanity. These were awarded to the five friends and to the General at a secret ceremony held in the White House. The children attended the ceremony, but were sorry that it had to be kept a secret. The President shook their hands and said, "You are five of the bravest and most resourceful children on our planet. Soon, when you help us liberate the world from the clutches of these evil invaders, we shall hold a public ceremony in your honor. Then the whole world will recognise you as the heroes that you are."

The children hearts swelled with pride and joy. Henry responded, "With the Chimp as our guide, the General as our ally and you supporting us, we are ready to take them on." The others all chorused, "This is only the beginning. Let us all together deliver the world from the forces of evil."

❖❖❖